The Silver Creek Secret

By

Christopher Doyle

To Kaylee...!
Happy Reading!
Christopher Doyle

This book is a work of fiction. Places, events, and situations in this story are purely fictional. Any resemblance to actual persons, living or dead, is coincidental.

ISBN: 1-4033-9280-3 (E-book)
ISBN: 1-4033-9281-1 (Paperback)
ISBN: 1-4107-0714-8 (Dust Jacket)

Library of Congress Control Number: 2002095575

This book is printed on acid free paper.

Printed in the United States of America
Bloomington, IN

1stBooks - rev. 02/13/03

Acknowledgements

The author wishes to thank the following people for their support and valuable input:
The Beverly Farms critique group—Pat Lowery Collins, Laurie Jacobs, Chris Jones, Donna McArdle, and Lenice Strohmeier; my editor Marcia Somerset; my school principal Dr. Paul Plante; and last, but not least, my students, past and present, who never cease to inspire me.

1.

After a long sleep, Kurt opened his eyes, the bright sun glaring in them. The rock beneath him was hard as brick, dry and dusty. At first, he moved only his fingers. Then slowly he stood up and stretched. His muscles were slightly stiff.

For a moment, he thought he had still been dreaming. He was no longer on Mount Catawalla in Ohio, gazing out at Milky Way Amusement Park, but on a very small, flat mountain in the middle of a desert. Tall, dark pines and thick, tree-like cactus studded the flat, dull landscape. A dry riverbed cut across the land like a giant scar. The distant mountains formed a jagged horizon all around him.

The wind whistled across the open plain. He heard a strange howling in the distance—a hungry, lonely sound. Kurt swallowed, his tongue sticking in his dry throat. This was not a dream, Kurt realized. A wave of panic surged through him.

He spotted a cluster of buildings about a half-mile away. He thought he heard voices, isolated shouts coming from that direction.

Were they really voices of people, he wondered, or was his mind playing tricks on him? He weighed in his mind what to do. If there were people living in those buildings, they might know the way back to Ohio.

Still unsure of what to do, he eased himself down the little mountain and began walking toward the cluster of buildings, the hard earth crackling

1

under his feet. The closer he got, the more the cluster took on the shape of an Old West town, much like the ones he had seen in many of his grandfather's photos. But there were no roads leading into the town, and no utility poles. Perhaps he had traveled back in time?

He picked up his pace, quickening into a jog. He wasn't much of a runner, and he had to slow down more than once to catch his breath.

The tiny town appeared to be deserted. Wooden buildings clustered around a dusty road. Metal signs swung and creaked in the wind. Kurt could still make out the words on some of them— "Sheriff's Office," and "Soda Shop," and "The Silver Creek Hotel."

Silver Creek? This couldn't be the same Silver Creek as the one in the story Pa told me, Kurt thought. He laughed out loud. His voice was the only one he heard. "Silver Creek," he said. "I'm in Silver Creek!"

A gaggle of laughing voices came from somewhere he couldn't pinpoint. He stopped and looked around, but he saw nobody. Some doors of houses were open, and some closed. One had a handcrafted sign that said "Welcome", something like what Ma would have made from the cover of a cake tin.

A woman came out from her small wooden house with a straw basket tucked under her arm, as if it were laundry she was about to hang. She stopped when she caught sight of Kurt, then hurried over to him.

"Roy?" she said. "It's Roy Sharp!" She covered her mouth with one hand and ran over to one of the houses and pounded on the door. "Patsy, open up!"

Roy Sharp? For some reason the name meant something to Kurt. Part of him wanted to say, "Yeah, it's me." But why would he? He'd always been Kurt Van Loon, for as long as he could remember—back to about age five.

There was a time when Kurt Van Loon had no name. His grandmother, Aberdine Robinson, often told Kurt the story of how she found him standing alone in Milky Way Amusement Park, holding a sticky cone and staring down at a puddle of ice cream at his feet. All he had for a name was "Kurt," which was printed on a nametag he had found on the ground. Mrs. Robinson tried to locate Kurt's parents, but he could not remember their names or even what they looked like. Mrs. Robinson and her husband Henry took the nameless five-year-old boy to the big comfortable farmhouse they shared with their grown daughter Helen and her husband Cliff Van Loon. The Van Loons finally adopted him, and that is how he became Kurt Van Loon. Kurt became attached to his new family, and the search for his real parents had ceased. As far as Kurt was concerned, he *was* home, and these *were* his real parents and grandparents.

But, try as he may, Kurt could not remember these events. Now, at age thirteen, he was beginning to have doubts about the truth of Ma's story.

"Patsy, open up!" the woman repeated, jolting Kurt out of his daydream.

A stocky woman with brown hair answered the door. "What is it, Muriel?"

3

"Roy is back!" Muriel cried, screeching like a seventh-grade girl.

Patsy gazed right in Kurt's direction and walked slowly toward him, her mouth partly open. She stopped right at his face. They were eye level.

"It really is you," she said. "Just look how much you've changed!"

That voice, Kurt thought, a raspy voice that sent a bell off in his brain. He knew this woman. But from where?

"Welcome back, honey," Patsy said. "We all missed you so much."

She put her arms around him and squeezed him. The embrace, although warm and welcoming, was choking him.

"But I'm—" he croaked out. She squeezed him tighter.

"I've got to tell the others," Muriel said, running to the hotel. "Palmer! Joanne! Roy's back! Our Roy has come home!" She kept beating on doors, and soon everyone was out in the open, forming a circle around him. They all wanted to touch him. The men were slapping his back, and the women were squeezing his hand and kissing him.

The children came running out, leaping and shouting with excitement. They froze in astonishment when they saw him.

"Roy?" one asked, his face twisted like a question mark.

"He's not Roy!" another said. "This kid's old."

"He just got bigger. That's all," said another.

"How can he get bigger?" the first one said. "We never got any bigger. And we've been here for years."

The crowd was quiet as the circle of faces looked at him intensely.

"You are Roy Sharp, aren't you?" a man with black and white hair asked, who responded to the name Palmer.

Before Kurt could think of an answer, a round lady with a big smile called from a wooden building by the Soda Shop. "Come on inside! We're gonna have this boy a party."

They sat him in the seat of honor, with the rest of the children sitting near his end of the long table. There were eight children in all, six boys and two girls. Most of them were ragged and dirty, but seemed happy and full of energy. They competed for his attention, telling jokes and pulling crazy stunts with their silverware. Two boys a little younger than him were probing at Kurt to open up.

"So where you been, Roy?"

"Did you get over the Edge?"

"How come you got older?"

"We thought the officials got you for sure."

"What's it like?"

"Is it dangerous like the grown-ups say?"

"Did you have to fight?"

"Tell us."

Kurt seemed to have already developed a sort of hero status with these kids, a feeling he'd never experienced before. "What makes you think I'm Roy?" he asked.

"See?" said one kid. "I told you he wasn't."

"He didn't say he wasn't," said another. "He just said—"

"I heard what he said. He's just being plain modest. Aren't you, Roy?"

5

Kurt smiled as he stuffed bread into his mouth to keep from talking.

The party was wonderful, with mouth-watering barbecued ribs and a big white fluffy cake for dessert. Huge family style serving platters were passed from hand to hand. Folks were chatting, laughing, and eating. Kurt counted thirty people including himself. Adults stole glances in his direction while talking with their neighbors. He wished he could hear what they were saying.

When dinner had wound down, and dirty plates remained untouched, a man wearing a silver badge and a Stetson stood up and tapped on his water glass for attention. The crowd grew quiet.

"As sheriff, let me be the first to welcome you back to Silver Creek, Roy," the man said in a low rumble.

The people burst into a round of applause and whistling cheers.

The sheriff removed his hat and held up his glass. "You must have no idea how much we've missed you, Roy, all these years. To see a young boy grow up while the rest of us in Silver Creek go unchanged, we are, of course, full of many questions. But rather than embarrass you, we would like to simply offer you our warmest welcome."

Unchanged? Kurt wondered. He remembered hearing one of the kids say the same thing.

The adults all lifted their glasses and said, "Hear! Hear!"

"I think Roy should give a speech," said one boy.

Some of the kids started to shout "Speech!" And then it all got louder, as they pounded on the table with their fists. "Speech! Speech! Speech! Speech!..."

Kurt stood up and grinned sheepishly. It was like he'd hit a power switch. The chatter stopped and everyone glued their attention onto him. He felt like he'd been swallowed. *Tell the truth*, he could hear Ma saying in his head.

Kurt licked his dry lips and told them. "I'm not Roy."

First there was a dead silence, like the first few seconds before a movie starts.

"What do you mean, you're not Roy?" a boy said.

"Who are you then?" said a girl.

"And how did you get here?" another asked.

"I'm Kurt," he said. "Kurt Van Loon, from Ohio."

Twenty-nine faces stared at him as if he'd just insulted them.

"I really don't know how I got here. Back home in Ohio I climbed this mountain, see. Mount Catawalla it's called. Since I was eight, I've climbed it every year on my birthday, and I try to beat my own record. Well, today's my thirteenth birthday, and I did make it to the top in record time. I had a great view of Milky Way Park and the Big Dipper roller coaster. But then I crashed and I must have blacked out, because, when I woke up, Milky Way Park was gone and I wasn't on Mount Catawalla anymore. I was on that mountain out there."

"The little one all by itself?" a boy asked.

"Yeah, that one," said Kurt. "So, I saw this town from out there, and I crossed the desert, thinking maybe I'd find somebody who could tell me how to get back to Ohio. Then, I see the sign for the Silver Creek Hotel, and I think to myself, this can't be the same Silver Creek as the one in my grandfather's

7

stories about the Old West. 'Cock-and-bull stories,' 'Ma called them. Here I was, thinking he'd made the whole thing up. But now that I meet you all, it's as if I already know you!"

He stepped away from his seat and went over to the lady with long dark hair. "You're Joanne, right?"

The woman chuckled. "Why, yeah."

He went over to the man with black and white hair. "And you're Palmer. You and Joanne run the hotel."

"That's right," the man said, nodding vigorously.

"So how does your grandpa know about us?" Joanne asked. "What's his name?"

Kurt chuckled. "Oh, I wouldn't say he knows you. You all are characters in the Silver Creek story he tells me all the time. Well, up until recently, that is. A few months ago, when I was outside helping him get his truck unstuck from a snow bank, he fell and started talking gibberish. When the doctor came, he said Pa had had a stroke. Now he's in a wheelchair, and he can't walk or talk. I still talk to him, and we still play checkers together, but it's not the same without his stories. Ma never believed them, but the way he talked about you made Silver Creek seem so real. I want so much to go back, so I can tell them I've actually been here! I know Pa would believe me. Oh, and his name is Henry Robinson."

A gasp went up over the adult crowd. The kids all had blank looks.

"Henry who?" a kid said.

"I remember him well," said Palmer. "He was here many summers ago. A young gentleman who

8

loved his family dearly. He woke up in the hotel, didn't know where he was."

"I found him in a corner room of the hotel," Joanne added. "He looked quite disoriented. When he asked me where he was, I told him he was in Silver Creek, and that this was the Silver Creek Hotel."

"Said he'd been in an accident and was taken to the hospital," said Palmer. "I told him we didn't have a hospital, but asked if could I bring him anything. He said he was hoping this was heaven, because he wanted to make sure his son Roy was okay. I told him I didn't know anything about heaven. Then he reached in his pocket and showed me a picture of Roy. I thought how much that black-and-white picture looked like Roy Sharp." Palmer went silent for awhile. He appeared to be struggling with a thought. "So, I went off to get Roy, but by the time we got back to the hotel, Mr. Robinson had gone."

"One minute he was resting peacefully on the bed in his room," Joanne explained, "and the next minute he'd vanished."

"Vanished?" Kurt repeated. That word had been part of his life since he could remember. He sat down, overcome with fear.

Kurt knew that, years ago, long before he came into the Robinson's lives, the Ma and Pa Robinson had a little boy named Roy. Young Henry Robinson loved his family, and he loved talking about the Old West. When Henry was a boy himself, his grandfather's collection of Old West artifacts had won first prize at the Ohio State Fair. Henry was so inspired that he dreamed of building his own Old West theme park someday.

9

Though Henry inherited a large farm from his parents, farm work didn't excite him too much. He and Aberdine finally decided to close the farm and build a family theme park based on the Old West.

There were over a dozen kiddie rides, a saloon that served up the best root beer floats around, and a stand where Aberdine served up mouth-watering morsels of chocolate chip cornbread. There was even a museum of Old West artifacts that had been passed down from Henry's grandfather.

No child ever left Robinson's Old West without a smile on his face. Families loved it. The Robinsons had never been happier.

Then one day the unthinkable happened. The Robinsons' little boy Roy disappeared. He was last seen riding the Bullet—the park's small, yellow roller coaster. Everyone figured he had been kidnapped, or worse.

The Robinsons were devastated. A cloud of gloom settled over the shrinking household. Henry wanted no more part of Robinson's Old West. He closed the park and sold off the land.

Kurt was jolted back to the present by Joanne's voice. "Well, no one actually *saw* Henry Robinson disappear," she was saying. "But there was no other way he could have left Silver Creek so quickly. It was just in a matter of minutes."

"He left the same way he came here?" Kurt asked slowly. "In a hotel room?"

"That's right," said Palmer.

"So, if I want to go home, all I've got to do is go back to the mountain?" Kurt asked.

"The rules are different for children," Palmer said in a smaller voice. "When Roy Sharp rode out to the Edge by himself, that was the last we saw of him. Probably got captured by authorities, or mauled to death by wild dogs."

Kurt stammered. "You mean, I might never go back?"

The sheriff rose slowly. The whole crowd was still as stone. The children looked as if they'd stopped breathing. "I'm afraid that might be true, Kurt."

2.

A boardwalk ran along in front of the hotel and soda shop. Kurt sat in a wooden chair on the boardwalk. An overhang above his head shielded him from the sun's bright rays. A building he thought to be the sheriff's office was shaded by trees and stood at the far side of the village. Small houses faced a footpath that wound around town. From a distance they looked well-made, even if they had been made entirely by hand. Maybe the people here had nothing better to do in the time they've been here. How long had they been here? Kurt wondered.

How long would he be here?

The people all went about their business. Palmer and Joanne tended to the hotel, possibly readying his room. He couldn't imagine what else they'd be doing. Silver Creek didn't seem to have any real visitors, except Kurt. If they ever did have visitors, they'd be here permanently. He wondered why they even needed a hotel.

The mountain on which he had awakened was visible from where he was sitting. Maybe I should go back and camp out there tonight, he thought. If Pa went back home from Silver Creek by lying back on his bed, there might be a chance Kurt could find his way back on the mountain.

He decided that he would spend the rest of the day checking out Silver Creek. Then by nightfall, after everyone had gone to bed, he would steal away quietly to the mountain to spend the night.

Ever since he arrived in Silver Creek, Kurt had an unquenchable thirst. It prickled his throat like a cactus. Next door was the soda shop. He decided to take a walk over.

The light inside the soda shop was dim, the floor gritty with sand. Mirrors covered some of the walls, and tall, swivel type stools were perched up close to the bar. A manual cash register was at one corner of the counter, and many kinds of glasses lined the shelves behind it—skinny ones for beer, fat deep ones for soda, even ones with metal handles for milk shakes. Somewhere a refrigerator hummed.

Kurt stood transfixed. A place with running electricity and metal fixtures all in a village that existed next to nowhere. Incredible, he thought.

"Are you thirsty, Mister Kurt," a male voice spoke.

Kurt turned his head. He had hardly noticed the hulking, black man in the white apron standing in the darkness. His arms folded over his chest, he took silent steps to the space behind the counter, and stared down at Kurt, his face cast in shadow. "What will it be?" His voice thundered. "You look like a root beer man."

"I don't have any money," said Kurt.

The man laughed. "Never mind. Sit down."

Kurt took a seat on a swivel stool.

The man slid aside a handle on a metal case in front of him, and pulled out a brown bottle, frosty and steaming like the way Kurt's breath hung frozen in the air on an icy winter day. He plunked a ball of white ice cream into a milk shake glass, popped the top off the bottle with his thumb and poured the root beer into it while stirring with a

13

glass rod that clinked against the sides. He pushed a straw inside it and set the glass on a small square napkin in front of Kurt.

"Drink up," he said.

Kurt had been so caught up in the fast, sweeping motions of this soda-making man, that he had forgotten how thirsty he was. He took a short sip from the straw. Then a long sip. Then he slurped continuously until he'd emptied half the glass. He let out a contented sigh.

"I'm not thirsty anymore," Kurt said in amazement.

The man grinned, his white teeth seeming to glow. "I'll bet you're always thirsty, too."

Kurt nodded. "How do you know so much about me?"

The man leaned on the counter, and gazed out the open door. "Every new kid who comes to Silver Creek is always thirsty. And I've never met a kid who didn't like root beer."

"Tell me about these kids," said Kurt. "But please first tell me your name."

"Dashiel." It was just one word, but the way it resonated in the room gave it meaning. Forceful, but friendly. Gripping the counter as if he intended to push it, Dashiel thought deeply. "The children came at various times," he said. "First was Roy Sharp. He was about this high," Dashiel positioned his hand a little higher than his waist. A laugh higher in pitch than Kurt expected came bubbling out of Dashiel like fizz from a shaken soda bottle. "We all wanted him, so we took turns. One week he would stay with me, one week with Patsy, one with Palmer, and so on."

"Everyone says I look like him," said Kurt.

14

"You resemble him," said Dashiel. "Obviously, you're much older than Roy was. But when you arrived in town, we all sensed that you were Roy. I think the people here are so tired of the same old thing, most of them keep wishing for something to change their lives. We missed Roy when we discovered he'd vanished."

"He wandered out by the Edge and got lost?" Kurt asked, remembering the rim of mountains.

"Last person to see him was Mr. Jackson who lives just on the other side of the mountains. I've never been to see him, none of us have too—risky a venture. But nothing stopped little Roy. Still don't know what made him ride out there on a donkey all alone. When Mr. Jackson came to visit us that one time years ago, he told us that Roy had stopped by his house asking for chocolate chip cornbread. After Mr. Jackson had fed him some and he'd asked Roy why he was leaving Silver Creek, Roy told him he was missing somebody." Dashiel became silent.

Chocolate chip combread? Kurt wondered. How funny! Ma Robinson was about the only person he knew that made the delectable treat. Thoughts of warm, buttery hunks of chocolate chip combread made Kurt's mouth water.

"When Roy got back on his donkey and rode off slowly," Dashiel continued. "Mr. Jackson saw the boy and his donkey disappear. Vanished into thin air, right before his eyes."

Kurt had never heard such a story. "Just like my grandfather did in the hotel. But that's impossible," he said. "How can someone vanish into thin air?"

Dashiel slowly swayed his head. "It's not how they disappear that's incredible. It's how they arrive

15

in Silver Creek in the first place. The children, I mean."

Kurt was glad Dashiel hadn't forgotten about the rest of the kids. "Did they pass out on a mountain like I did?"

Dashiel's laughter came again like fizzy soda exploding from a bottle. "Why don't you ask them yourself? They'll give you a much better story than I ever could." Dashiel reached out his long hand and gave Kurt's a powerful shake that sent vibrations up his entire arm. Then he handed Kurt the clean, empty root beer bottle. "Give this to the kids. Stop by again."

It wasn't until Kurt left the soda shop that he realized how strange that last sentence was. Of course, he'd be by again. He would most likely be here for the rest of his life.

Kurt hurried over to an open area where some of the children were knocking metal soda cans over with a rock.

"Stand back!" one of the boys shouted to Kurt. A girl about ten was about to hurl a ball of cloth at a line of root beer bottles from a good ten paces away. She reeled and pitched. Several bottles wobbled and toppled onto the sand.

"I'm ahead!" she cheered.

Kurt held the root beer bottle out to one of the older boys, about eleven. "Here's one more from Dashiel."

"Hey, Kurt," the boy said. "I'm George. This is Haley Dawn." He indicated the girl with freckles and a tight-lipped grin.

"This is Hoochie," he added, at which a boy of about eight touched the brim of his hat and nodded.

16

"And this is W.D." The kid called W.D. simply grinned.

"What do your initials stand for?" Kurt asked.

"Whistling Dixie," George said. "Show him, W.D."

From that boy's lips came the most creative melody Kurt had ever heard, a cross somewhere between "Amazing Grace" and the Beatles' "Yesterday".

Kurt's jaw dropped open in amazement. The kids all joined him in applause.

"He's never told us his real name," said George. "He hasn't spoken a word since he's been here. Guess that's why he's such a good friend." He put his arm around W.D. and smiled.

"How long have you all been here?" Kurt asked the group.

George and W.D. looked at one another and shrugged. "About forty years, maybe," said George.

"I think I've been here thirty," said Haley Dawn.

"About twenty for me," said Hoochie.

Kurt laughed. "How could you all have been here that long? We're only kids. You're even younger than me."

"No we're not," said George. "We just never got older."

"Yeah, in Silver Creek, kids stay kids forever," said Haley Dawn.

"That's okay with me," said Hoochie. "I wouldn't want to be a grown-up. Boring!"

"And now that you're here, you won't get older either," George said to Kurt.

I could stay the same forever, Kurt thought. But then Ma and Pa would miss me. But how would I get back? What if camping out on the mountain didn't work? What was Pa's secret? How did he get back to the real world?

W.D. waved his hand in front of Kurt's face and whistled.

"I think we're losing him," said George, laughing at Kurt.

"How did you get here anyway?" Hoochie asked.

"I woke up there on that mountain," he answered, pointing behind him.

"What mountain?" George asked.

Kurt turned around to look, and the others turned with him. But they were all staring at an empty desert. The mountain had vanished.

Kurt ran out into the open desert. "It's gone!" he screamed. "Where's the mountain? Where did it go?" He dropped to his hands and knees onto the sand. His whole body trembled.

The other kids ran out and stood by his side. "Are you all right, pal?" George asked.

"Are you having a heart attack?" Hoochie asked.

Kurt shook his head, although he felt like he'd just been to the edge of a cliff and looked down. "It was there," he said, his voice shaking. "I swear it was there."

"Take it easy, pal," George said, kneeling on the ground beside him. And when he did, so did the others.

"I don't get this place," said Kurt. He looked at each kid, one at a time, squarely in the eyes. "What is this place? Where am I?"

"Silver Creek," Haley Dawn chirped.

He turned on her. "I *know* it's Silver Creek!"

She backed away and her eyes became pools of tears.

"I'm sorry," said Kurt. He felt his own eyes beginning to sting. "I just wish I knew where I was."

"If it's any help," said George, "we don't know where we are either."

Kurt stared at him intensely. "I want to know how you all got here."

The kids exchanged glances for support. The two younger ones begged George with their eyes for him to be the first to speak. W.D., the boy who couldn't speak, glared quietly at George, as if he were sending George all his thoughts, telling him what to say.

George lowered his head, as if he were going to be sick. "I don't really remember how I got here. The first thing I remember about this place is I was walking across the desert by myself, and I was really thirsty. I wasn't far from the mountains. Then I heard this whistling from far off. I saw a kid out by another part of the mountains, and he was walking toward me, waving his arms like crazy over his head. I ran to him and when I saw his face, I recognized him, but I couldn't remember who he was. It was the weirdest thing, as if I'd known him my whole life.

"I said to him, 'Don't I know you?' He just shrugged and gave me that goofy grin of his. He said absolutely nothing. I said, 'Where are we?' Then he made a sign with his hands to get me to follow him. We walked for awhile toward the other edge of the mountains, and I said, 'Don't you talk?' He said nothing and then started whistling this weird song. We saw this village in the distance, and we started running toward it. And when we got there, Dashiel made us root beer floats. There was another kid in the Soda Shop—a little kid, about

19

five, named Roy Sharp. He was slurping on the same kind of drink, and he looked really happy."

George went silent for a long while, then sat back with his legs stretched out in front of him.

W.D. was biting his lip, his eyes fixed on something invisible.

Hoochie had his hands on his knees, his eyeballs quivering.

Haley Dawn sighed, tracing the sand with her fingers.

Kurt got abruptly to his feet, and stepped out of the circle. He gazed out at the distant mountains. "Did you ever try to go back?"

"We can't!" said Hoochie. "My guardians always told me, 'Don't you ever go out there, Hoochie. Remember how Roy went out there and never came back?' They say Roy was eaten by dholes."

Kurt's concentration broke. He turned and laughed. "Dholes? What are they?"

"Wild dogs," said Hoochie. "You can hear them sometimes at night if they're close. But they're usually a long way off. In the mountains."

"Have you ever seen one?" Kurt asked.

"Not me," said Hoochie. The others shook their heads as well.

"No one's ever really seen them," said George. "When Mr. Jackson came to see us one time to tell us about Roy disappearing, I asked him what that dog-sound was. He told us they were dholes, and that they were dangerous. He told us the officials at the Edge trap them and train them to kill people who try to sneak past the mountains."

"Dashiel told me Roy didn't get killed though," said Kurt. "He said Mr. Jackson saw him disappear into thin air. Just like that mountain did. Have you ever seen anything disappear?"

W.D. nodded vigorously.

"Get out, W.D.!" said George. "What did you ever see disappear?"

W.D. scrambled to his feet and began making a waving and diving motion with his hand. He made a whistling sound like the falling embers of exploded fireworks.

George gave his friend a shove. "You're lying! You're making all this up!"

W.D. pushed him back and after a few more pushes, they were on the ground, rolling, each trying to pin the other.

Kurt got down and pried their shoulders apart. Soon the three of them were sitting on the ground, the two younger boys covered in light brown dirt and eyeing each other spitefully.

Haley Dawn stood over them. "Why are you fighting? You guys are friends."

"You're both gonna be here forever," said Hoochie. "You'd be stupid to stay mad at each other. Shake hands and make up."

At first, the two boys refused to face each other. They were still breathing hard from the combat. Kurt got them both to stand up. "Come on, you two. So, W.D. saw something disappear."

"I don't believe him," said George. "He's lying."

W.D. scowled at him, forming a fist.

"How can someone lie when they can't even talk?" said Haley Dawn.

George glared at W.D., but there was a wide space like a canyon between them. "I bet he could talk if he really wanted to. He's just being a jerk."

21

George turned and walked away in a huff back toward the village.

"Is it true you can't talk at all, W.D.?" Kurt asked.

The short-haired whistler seemed embarrassed. He looked like a flesh-colored statue, his face streaked with gritty sand, his dingy shirt rippling in the wind. In his silence, W.D. made it very clear that even if he could speak, he sure wasn't about to do so.

Kurt wandered a short distance away and gazed out at the jagged horizon. He immersed himself in the dry, marvelous scenery. Despite all the magical events that had taken place there, Silver Creek seemed like any other desert location he'd read about.

He heard the two younger children scrape their feet along the ground to stand behind him.

"What do you think he saw disappear, Kurt?" Hoochie asked.

Kurt was immersed in thought. He imagined W.D.'s rising and diving hand motion and the accompanying whistle. "Has to be something that flies. Something that moves through the air." He watched and listened to the empty blue sky. "You guys ever see airplanes?"

"I know what airplanes are," said Hoochie.

"So do I," said Haley Dawn. "I just can't remember what they look like."

3.

Nightfall came at around the time that Kurt expected. He wasn't one to wear a watch, but that evening, when all the kids (all but George) had circled around a small fire, he had a burning desire to know.

"Do you know what time it is, Eddie?" he asked.

"No one keeps time here," the ten-year-old answered. "There's no need to, since no one in Silver Creek ever has to be anywhere."

"Don't you guys get bored?" Kurt asked.

"What's bored?" a girl named Tiffany asked. She was sitting next to Haley Dawn.

All the kids gazed at Kurt, as if he were the only one who knew. Their faces were bathed in orange from the fire.

"How could you not know?" Kurt asked in amazement. "It's when you want something fun to happen, but you wait, and you wait. And nothing happens."

"What's fun?" a boy named Daniel asked. He was sitting next to Hoochie and seemed to be the youngest of the group.

At first, Kurt was unable to respond. Then he laughed. "This is a joke, right? A joke on the new kid! Well, you really had me for a second. I really thought you all were being serious."

"Why would we kid about something we didn't know?" Eddie asked.

Kurt rubbed his tired face. How could these kids not know what fun was? He felt very sorry for them. He thought for a moment.

"You know that game you all were playing with the root beer bottles? You liked what you were playing, didn't you?"

"Sure, we do," said Haley Dawn. "We play that game every day."

Kurt's spirits were lifting. "There you go. That's what you call fun. Now, what else do you do that you like?"

Kurt was worried when it took almost a full minute before someone else spoke up.

"We like flicking little shiny rocks," said Stephen, Hoochie's other friend. He pulled some out of his pocket and held them out for Kurt to see.

"Marbles!" Kurt was delighted. "You guys like to play with marbles. That's great!" At the same time, though, Kurt was amazed that they didn't know the correct word for those little shiny rocks. "All right, so we've got the bottle game and marbles. I suppose you don't have TV or radio."

All he got were blank stares. Kurt felt the need to explain himself again. "A TV is a box that you plug in, and you get a picture."

"Yes!" a shout went up. Hoochie was on his feet. "I don't have one, but I know who does. Palmer. It's got a picture of Roy Sharp in it."

"That's a picture frame, dummy," said Eddie.

It saddened Kurt to see these kids this way. Back at home, he wasn't rich by any means, but Ma and Pa had TV, and Kurt had his own stereo headset. Clearly, these kids were trapped in the past and had never known these modern

24

conveniences. Still, he expected them to know the difference between fun and boredom.

"I wish I could take you all back to Ohio with me," said Kurt. "We have everything. TV, CD players, movie theaters, video games, paintball. It's impossible to be bored."

"Really?" Haley Dawn said excitedly. "That's sounds like—what you said—fun."

"Where's Ohio?" Stephen asked. "Is that on the other side of the Edge?"

"Everywhere but Silver Creek is over the Edge," said Eddie. "And the Edge is too dangerous to even go near it."

"How do you know?" Kurt asked. "Just because the grown-ups tell you something is scary?"

"Our guardians tell us there are officials who will kill us if we try to cross the mountains," said Haley Dawn.

"And there are big wild dogs, too, called dholes, and they eat people," Tiffany added.

"But just think," said Kurt. "If every place is on the other side of those mountains, I could take you all back to Ohio with me just by us crossing the Edge. So, it might be risky. We won't know till we find out. And we'll all go together."

The children looked at one another for agreement. Their faces seemed to convey that this is what they'd been wanting for a long time, for someone like them to have enough courage to be their leader, to tell them about good things that existed in another place.

Silver Creek was dark by the time Kurt headed for the hotel for the night. He watched as his friends broke away toward their own dwellings.

25

Christopher Doyle

Kurt learned that each of the children in Silver Creek lived with one or two guardians, and hoped that they wouldn't be in trouble for being out at night.

The door to the hotel was open, and a light was on inside, illuminating the front desk. Kurt stepped in, and listened quietly. The rest of the hotel was dark.

"Palmer?" he called. "Joanne?" He remembered that these were the folks who took care of the hotel.

Hearing no answer, he slowly guided himself down the short hallway, and found some stairs. They creaked as he climbed them, feeling for them with his feet. A window on the second floor let in enough light from the brightly moonlit sky to enable him to see more clearly. He counted eight rooms, four on either side of the hallway.

He entered the first room. There was a single bed, which made a crackling sound when he sat on it, a large window covered by a wooden shutter, and a writing desk with drawers deep enough to hold clothing. He pulled open the shutter to let in the fresh air and lay down on the bed.

He stretched out completely on the mattress, and found it to be fairly comfortable, even if it was noisy when he shifted around. The wind outside whirred softly, lightly tapping the shutter against the wall in a quiet rhythm that soothed him.

His eyes grew accustomed to the darkness, and the moonlight gave the walls a pale yellow cast. He ran his hand along the wall near the bed, touching upon what felt like a carving. Feeling the grooves, his fingers spelled out the first few letters in the carving, R-O-Y. He struggled to see the carved writing in the dim light, and continued following

26

the engraving with his fingers. He kept at it until he could decipher the entire message: "Roy Sharp was here."

4.

After a fitful sleep, Kurt dragged himself off the bed and stumbled to the window. This was his morning ritual at home, and for just a brief second, he had forgotten where he was.

The kids were already up, some riding their horses. Those little dirtbags, he thought. Apparently, horseback riding didn't count as something fun. They moved those horses like kids back home pulled stunts on skateboards. The best Kurt could do with a horse was climb up on Pa's old pony Rusty and walk him around the yard. Even that was a challenge.

He was right about the walls. They were yellow. He spotted the message on the wall. Kurt remembered doing the same thing once on a tree on top of Mount Catawalla back home. Awhile back, he had scratched his name everywhere—the picnic bench near the pond at Milky Way Park, the arm of Pa's old reading chair in the spare bedroom, inside his desk at school. For some reason, he'd always had an insatiable need to let people know who he was.

And he thought it was quite remarkable that a boy who resembled him so much seemed to have the same desire.

"You sleep well, Kurt?" Palmer asked, appearing in the doorway in dull gray and brown clothes.

"Palmer, do you have a picture of Roy Sharp? One of the kids told me you did."

"Not of Roy Sharp, but of Roy Robinson. I have it on the front desk downstairs. Come on down."

The hotel looked much less interesting, less spooky, in the daytime. All the blacks had turned to light browns that made Kurt yawn.

Palmer leaned against the big desk by the front door and handed Kurt the framed black and white photo. "That's Roy Robinson. 'Course I didn't know that at the time. When your grandpa was here and he showed me Roy's picture, I couldn't get over the likeness. I was so excited, I went and got Roy Sharp, telling him I needed his help in the hotel. I wanted it to be a surprise for the two of them. 'Course they never did get to see each other."

Kurt's head felt as if it was full of sand. He was having a hard time keeping track of the two Roys. "Wait a second. How did Roy Sharp get here in the first place?"

"He rode into Silver Creek on a donkey, cute as could be. He was the first child ever to set foot in this village. Although we were delighted to welcome him, we were a little sad, too, just knowing he must have come here the same way we did."

"How was that?" Kurt asked.

Palmer looked hesitant for a moment, and closed the door. "We're all dead. At least all of us adults here. I'm not so sure about the kids."

For a second Kurt wondered if he was still dreaming. "You're all dead? How could you be dead? You're standing right here, talking to me." Then he started to laugh, but Palmer wasn't laughing.

"Think of how you got here," said Palmer. "At the party you told us how you passed out on some mountain back home, and that somehow you woke

29

up on top of another mountain and found yourself here."

Kurt couldn't move. His mind was making the connection, but he didn't want to admit it. "But I can't be dead," he said, little more than his lips moving. "You said the rules were different for kids."

"How old are you?" Palmer asked.

"Thirteen yesterday."

"You're the oldest kid in this town. Somehow you must count for an adult."

Kurt wasn't ready to be an adult. He started to think this place was some kind of cruel trick. He had to just be having a bad dream.

Kurt shook his head. "There's no way I'm dead."

He stepped past Palmer and opened the door and walked out of the hotel.

"Just the same, Kurt. We're all glad you're here," said Palmer.

Kurt stopped just on the other side of the threshold and turned and looked at Palmer, who appeared apologetic.

"It's really not a bad place," said Palmer.

Kurt shook his head. "The kids here don't even know what it means to have fun or be bored. You can't tell me they're not bored. They can't even remember what their lives were like before they came here."

When it appeared that Palmer had no more to say, Kurt continued walking. At first he didn't know where he was going, but he found himself heading in the direction of the sheriff's office, a small gray house at the far end of the village. He glanced at the photo of the cute little kid with the impish grin. "If you can hear me, Roy, whichever Roy you are, help me get out of this mess, will you?"

The little office was shaded by small trees with twisted trunks and thick, dark green leaves. A short stone path led up to the door. Kurt knocked on the heavy wooden door and waited.

On the door was a round copper plate with the word "Welcome" etched into it. Its border was made up of tiny decorative dents that resembled bunches of grapes. A wind chime played in the breeze. Four round bars of metal, possibly silver, clanged heavily, sounding like church bells.

Kurt studied the photo in his hand. It was covered with a small square of glass held in a metal frame. He remembered the good silverware that Ma used when she had the pastor and friends from church over on occasional Sundays. The forks, knives, and spoons she used on such days were less shiny than the ones she used every day, and much heavier. Kurt recognized the metal frame in his hand to be that of silver. And when he turned it over, he saw a name etched in the corner: "Dan Calloway."

If his memory served him right, that had to be the sheriff Pa had told him about in his stories about Silver Creek.

Kurt knocked loudly.

"Hello, Mr. Van Loon." The greeting came not from inside the house but from the narrow road that wound through town. The sheriff, who had long silver hair and a beard, was waving to him. "I was just going out to check on the fences. Would you like to come along? There are several small horses in the stable you can choose from."

Kurt followed the sheriff to the long, open barnlike building and selected a brown pony with white spots. The sheriff saddled him up and Kurt hoisted himself on.

The riding felt awkward and bumpy, like one of those old kiddie rides at Milky Way Park. He wobbled as the pony struggled to keep up behind the sheriff's tall steed. He tucked the picture frame into his shirt, so he could hold onto the reins with both hands.

As they passed through the village, Kurt caught sight of some of the residents going about their business, waving to the sheriff and him as they rode by.

"Morning, Miss Ruth," the sheriff called to a woman in a loose floral dress. "Painting your house again? Isn't that the third time this year?"

She laughed. "Who's counting, Dan?" Her house stood out from the others. It was a soft blue. Half of one wall had already been painted with different colored flowers on trailing vines. When Kurt looked at them quickly, they looked like real vines covering the side of her house.

The houses were close so that the residents could converse with their neighbors, but far enough part to give each its own identity. Except for small foot paths, there seemed to be no boundaries separating the properties.

"Where are these fences you're checking on?" Kurt called to the sheriff who was still ahead of him.

The sheriff pointed in the direction of tall cactus off in the distance. Kurt could just make out a series of wooden posts just past them, sticking up out of the ground. They seemed like guards in a line that stretched in both directions.

When they finally got past the buildings, Kurt could see farther into distance all around. The fences cornered off and formed right angles on both sides. Glancing behind, Kurt could barely make out the outline of the fence on the other side of town.

"How much fence is there?" Kurt asked, when he finally caught up with the sheriff.

"Three thousand yards running north to south, and five thousand running east to west. About fifty thousand acres total."

No wonder he never noticed the fences when he first arrived in Silver Creek. They were a long way off. Fifty thousand acres was huge. His grandparents lived on two hundred acres, a good-sized lot of land, even for rural Ohio. They used to have even more. Milky Way Park, which was about twice that size, used to be part of their land.

"Is the fence there for a reason?" Kurt asked.

"To keep out wild critters mostly. It's been here longer than we have. Whoever was here before us must have been ranchers who built them to keep their cattle from running off."

"How long have you lived here? Were you the first one?"

The sheriff smiled to himself. "It's hard to say exactly. For as long as I can remember is the best answer I can give you. I *was* the first one in Silver Creek. I was riding Foreigner here," he said, indicating his horse, "when I happened upon this place. It reminded me of an old mining outpost, with a sparkling creek running by it. A mighty peculiar thing to see in the desert, I thought. Being thirsty I took a drink, and realized the banks of the creek had traces of silver and copper in them."

"But the creek's gone," Kurt interrupted. "When I came here, the creek bed was dry."

"That's because it just hasn't rained in a while," said the sheriff.

"For how long?"

"A couple of years."

"A couple of years? Wouldn't you all die without water?"

The sheriff was silent. Kurt began to remember what Palmer had said earlier that morning, that all the adults in Silver Creek were already dead. What would dead people need with water anyway?

"You sure are a curious son-of-a-gun, aren't you, boy?" said the sheriff.

Finally, they reached the fence. Kurt's bottom felt like he'd been sitting on top of a flagpole.

"You want to check for any breaks in the fence. Keep your eye out for any loose wire, too. Look for clumps of hair and traces of blood, any evidence that an animal's been trying to get through. This here's the east. We'll both head in opposite directions and meet all the way back at the west end. Then we'll ride back to town."

Kurt felt overwhelmed. "But that will take hours."

"No, it won't. About an hour and a half if you keep moving. I've done the whole thing myself in two hours. I've got pliers here in the saddle bag, but for today why don't you just keep an eye out for parts of the fence that need checking. Make a mental note of the things I told you." Then he turned his horse and headed off in the southerly direction.

Kurt sighed. He had gotten nowhere with the sheriff. There was still much more he needed to know.

He slid off the pony and sat down slowly against a post to ease his discomfort. He took the photo from his shirt and gazed at it. "I don't know, Roy. It sure doesn't feel like you're helping me out here."

Then out of the sky, came the first bird he'd seen in Silver Creek. It alighted several fence posts away. It was of the most amazing colors Kurt had ever seen. It looked something like a jungle bird, with iridescent green, blue, red, and gold feathers, and a long plumed tail. It gave a series of long, piercing cries.

Kurt felt elated. He no longer thought about his sore bottom. Ever since his mountain disappeared, this had been the first magical thing that had happened to him in Silver Creek. And when he looked off toward the northern desert, he saw what had long eluded him. His mountain had reappeared, only now it was shimmering, just like a photograph in which a second picture was superimposed onto another. He glanced down at Roy's picture, and for a moment, he saw himself.

5.

The exotic bird was as still and calm as a house pet. Kurt walked softly over to it and kept a respectful distance, fearful of alarming it.

"What kind of bird are you?" Kurt asked it.

The bird cocked its head to one side, and to the other. Kurt knew it was looking right at him, aware that since a bird's eyes are on the sides of its head, it could only see Kurt by looking sideways.

It gave another series of long, piercing cries, the same call as it had made to him a moment ago.

"Are you trying to tell me something?" said Kurt. He waited in silence. Aware that a bird could never respond in English, Kurt would have to rely on some other means of communication. But what?

Kurt gazed at the mountain, still shimmering like a thin cloud. At times, it seemed to not be there at all. The bird, however, seemed very real. He wished he could touch it.

"I want to go back to the mountain, bird," Kurt said. "I don't even know why I'm here in this crazy place. You look pretty lost here yourself. You look like you belong in a rainforest, not in a desert.

"I don't know about this sheriff. I can't believe he wanted me, a new kid, to ride the whole fence. Can you imagine it, bird? Eight thousand yards of fence. That's almost five miles, isn't it? I'm not riding five miles. He can—"

A sudden gunshot scared the devil out of him. He dropped to his knees and covered his head. It was the first gunfire he'd heard in Silver Creek. Maybe it was those officials. He didn't think he was that close to the Edge. The mountains were still a long way off.

What would anyone be shooting at? he wondered. Everyone here was dead, at least from what folks had told him.

He thought for sure the bird had flown away. But when he looked up, it was still perched there, cool and collected.

Kurt reached out with his finger and gently stroked the bird's shiny back. "Say, maybe you're dead, too." Kurt started to laugh at the foolishness of the thought. "Yeah, right," he answered himself. "A dead bird in Silver Creek. No wonder that gunshot didn't scare you.

The bird flew and landed on Kurt's shoulder. The closeness of the multicolored feathers tickled his cheek.

Kurt glanced at Roy's photo, the bird still perched on his shoulder. "All right, Roy," Kurt said to the picture. "This is too dangerous a place to hang around. Let's get out of here." He slipped the picture into his shirt, placed one foot in the stirrup, and hoisted himself into the saddle.

He headed the horse back toward the village. There was no use in continuing around the entire northern half of the fence. He wasn't even all that curious about what he'd be missing. Probably nothing. Heck, getting this bird for a birthday present was going to be pretty tough to beat.

As Kurt watched the shimmering mountain, he began to have the strangest feeling. He started to feel light. The sun seemed to be getting brighter and bigger, so big that it was swallowing him up—horse, bird, and all.

The next thing Kurt knew, which was probably less than a second later, the sun had gone back to its usual brightness. Kurt was still on the horse, the bird on his shoulder. Only now, he was right beside the mountain.

He looked up at it in wonder. Although from this vantage point, it did not seem to shimmer a whole lot. He figured he must have traveled several miles.

"Oh, my gosh!" he cried. "Oh, my gosh, oh, my gosh! What just happened to me?"

The bird took flight into the village. Kurt flew into a panic and rolled off the horse, nearly spraining his ankle.

"Hey, wait!" Kurt called. He ran after it, hollering. "Wait!" *Why didn't I take track in junior high?* he grumbled to himself.

The bird flitted rather like a hummingbird. A strange way to fly for such a graceful-looking bird, Kurt thought. But then, this place was strange all around. A soda shop in the desert. A dry creek. A mountain that disappears and then reappears. A bird that helps you get from one place to another without moving.

It's a wonder I'm not going out of my mind, he thought.

The bird alighted on top of the hotel. Perched on its roof it looked a little like a weathervane. Kurt gazed up at it, out of breath. "Please don't leave me," he called to his feathered companion.

"There you are, Quester!" a woman's voice scolded from behind Kurt. "You come down from there this instant, sweetie." It was Miss Ruth, the

38

woman in the flowing, flowered dress Kurt had seen on his journey to the fence with the sheriff.

The bird flew to Miss Ruth's outstretched arm. "He's still new at this messenger business," she said to Kurt, stroking the bird's shiny back.

"Messenger?" Kurt asked.

"Yes, I sent him to bring you back here, Kurt. You shouldn't be letting Dan talk you into riding fence with him. For the love of Pete, you're a guest in Silver Creek."

"A guest?" Kurt repeated. "You mean, I'm not staying?"

"Come on inside. I'll fix you some rose hip tea."

Kurt followed her along the narrow winding footpath to her house. Bright red and yellow desert flowers grew in clusters in her yard. Silver wind chimes along the edge of her house, like the one at the sheriff's office, played like music boxes in the breeze.

Her house inside was bright and richly decorated. Quilts covered much of the sitting furniture. A short-haired gray cat lazed on the back of the sofa, curling its tail. It didn't seem to bother the bird.

"There you are," Miss Ruth said gently, guiding the bird to its cageless perch. "And I've got a special treat for you today." She placed what appeared to be some special seeds in the bird's feed box. There was something like a clubhouse for the bird, as well as a swinging bar, a pine tree branch, and even a working waterfall.

"Lucky bird," Kurt said as Miss Ruth prepared the tea in her small pantry. "Where did you find it?"

"Quester found me," Miss Ruth answered. "Back when the creek was full to overflowing. So many

39

beautiful and strange creatures came to drink and swim in the river. When the creek dried up, all the animals and birds went away. But this one kept coming back. Must have been the flowers in the garden."

"How did you come up with the name Quester for a bird?" Kurt asked, settling onto the sofa, and stroking the cat's warm fur. It closed its eyes and purred. "Does the cat have a name, too?"

Miss Ruth emerged from the pantry, carrying a tray with a ceramic teapot and cups, and a sugar bowl with a tiny spoon in it. She set it on the coffee table in front of them, and sat in a fancy high-back chair.

"Quester got his name, because he would go off for days at a time sometimes and then come back, just like he'd been on a quest for something. I would wonder where he'd gone. And that's Glenda," she added, indicating the cat. "I've had her since the Flood. That's a figure of speech, you know."

"I know," said Kurt, watching her pour the steaming tea. "It means the Noah's ark flood. My Ma says that all the time. Tell me more about Quester," he added politely. "You told me he was new at the messenger business."

"That's right," said Miss Ruth. "I send him off every now and then to let me know if rain is coming. If he stretches out and ruffles his feathers, that's his sign. Sometimes he brings back special things for me, like this tea. Rose hips, as you might know, do not grow in the desert but by the seashore. Quester here somehow found his way to the seashore, because one morning as I was opening my door, I found a box of rose hip tea on my front walk. And there was Quester, looking all proud and satisfied with himself." She took a quiet sip from her cup. "And now he's brought you here."

Kurt felt anxious inside, wanting to understand Silver Creek. Was he only a guest, like she said, or was he dead, like Palmer had told him?

"Something troubling you, sweetie?" Miss Ruth asked. "Drink some of your tea. It soothes the spirit."

Kurt drank some of the warm tea. It had a bittersweet taste, somewhat like peaches and raspberries. "Am I dead, Miss Ruth?"

"Pardon?"

"Palmer told me I was dead. Is he lying?"

"You're only a boy. Why on earth would you be dead? Only the grown-ups here are dead. The children are..." Her voice trailed off as she took another sip of tea. Now she looked lost in thought.

"What?" Kurt asked.

"Missing," she said.

There was a long silence. Kurt set down his cup on the coffee table. "Missing? From where?"

"I don't know. That's just what I've been told." She had broken eye contact with him.

Kurt pressed on. The need to know was eating at him. "Who told you?"

Miss Ruth began to look irritated. "Somebody, something. I don't know. I can't remember!" She set down her cup, and touched her forehead with one hand, as if she had a headache.

"Maybe I better go," said Kurt. As he got up from the couch, the cat leaped down to the floor by his feet.

"Kurt, sweetie," Miss Ruth said, rising quickly from her chair. "I don't want you to think I'm hiding anything from you. I really don't know. None of us

41

really know why we're here. Maybe...." She avoided his stare again.

"Maybe what?" Kurt asked.

She appeared to be searching for the right words. "Maybe you're here to tell us."

6.

Kurt walked out of Miss Ruth's house, totally frustrated. The adults in this stupid town were beginning to get on his nerves. So far each one—Dashiel, Palmer, the sheriff, and Miss Ruth—had each told him only a part of their story. They were all keeping some truth hidden from him, and Kurt was losing his patience.

He felt a twinge of guilt for leaving Miss Ruth's house so abruptly. Ma would have scolded him for being rude.

He started toward the soda shop. The tea hadn't done much to ease his thoughts. He pulled the framed photo from his shirt and gazed at it as he walked. "I've got to get out of this place, Roy," Kurt said to the picture.

He remembered that he'd left his horse by the shimmering mountain, and thought he'd check up on him. But when he reached the soda shop, he saw that the mountain was no longer there. It had vanished again.

Kurt hurled the photo at the ground, shattering the glass. "Roy Sharp, why are you doing this to me?"

Dashiel appeared in the doorway and stooped to pick up the picture. He showed it to Kurt. The glass had a starburst crack from the center outward.

"The sheriff can fix this," he said.

Kurt cringed at the thought of the sheriff, who must have been fiercely angry with him for abandoning his job.

"You look disturbed, Mister Kurt. Come inside and have a root beer."

Kurt took the photo back and followed Dashiel into the cool shop. George was sitting at the bar, sipping a soda. Kurt went over and sat on the stool next to him. George gave Kurt a cold sideward glance.

"You wouldn't believe what happened to me today," Kurt whispered to George.

George seemed barely interested as he played with the straw in his glass. "You saw something disappear."

"Not exactly. I rode out with the sheriff to the fence, because he asked me to help him look for places that needed mending. We had just gone our separate ways, when I felt really tired and had to sit down. What did I see but this cool-looking bird, at least four different colors, like it came straight out of some rainforest. I look off in the distance, and what do I see but the mountain I told you about that had disappeared. Only now it was shimmering, like it wasn't quite there. The bird climbs up on my shoulder, and the next thing I know, I'm transported back there to the mountain."

George looked as if Kurt were completely out of his mind. "You and W.D. You're both crazy."

"You think *I'm* crazy?" Kurt whispered so Dashiel wouldn't hear. "Just ask the grown-ups in this place how they got to Silver Creek. None of them can give you a straight answer. Palmer says the adults are all dead. Miss Ruth says the kids are all missing. The sheriff—"

44

"What do you mean, the kids are all missing?" George said.

Kurt raised his hands in surrender. "I have no clue."

In his mind, Kurt flashed back to the day he climbed Mount Catawalla and gazed out at Milky Way Park. The sun dancing on the steel fixtures made the whole place sparkle. There was a sense of magic about it, as if he had been hoisted onto someone's shoulders to catch a glimpse of heaven.

The park was the biggest in Ohio and home to the most thrilling roller coaster east of the Mississippi—The Big Dipper. The space-like coaster took hairpin turns that would scare the hair off one's head. Since the park was built forty years ago, eight children in all had disappeared while riding The Big Dipper. Some had been with friends, others with parents. Fellow riders screamed in horror as they exited the main tunnel and discovered that their companions had vanished.

The children had all been between the ages of five and eleven when they vanished. Each time someone disappeared, the ride was closed down for legal inspection but was always found to be flawless. After the first disappearance, park visitors shied away from the coaster. The park considered tearing down the ride for good, but its patrons protested. The Big Dipper stayed and was updated several years back. Now it was the most state-of-the-art roller coaster in the country.

Kurt had always wondered what happened to those eight kids....

Dashiel set a generous root beer float in front of Kurt. "Have you thought about exploring the Edge?"

Kurt glanced at George. "We talked about it. Well, George wasn't there, but the rest of the kids were. And they're all curious about it. None of them can remember the last time they had any real fun. Of course, everyone around here says the Edge is a dangerous place."

Dashiel smiled. "How old are you?"

"Thirteen, yesterday."

"How long are you going to listen to crazy adults? If you want to go to the Edge, then go to the Edge. See what you find. No one's actually been there before. They're all too scared. All because Roy Sharp never came back. Those stories about the officials, and the vicious dogs..." Dashiel shrugged.

"You mean, it's all made up?" Kurt asked.

"Could be," Dashiel answered. "But if you don't take risks, you don't gain anything. I've always believed that." He slapped the counter, and walked off through the doorway in the back of the room.

The two boys sat alone in silence.

"Dashiel's right," said Kurt. "We need to prove these grown-ups wrong. We've got to go to the Edge and see what's there. Maybe even see what's on the other side."

"But our guardians are just trying to protect us," said George.

"Protect us from what? Something made Roy Sharp go to the Edge, and he was only five."

"But look what happened to him."

"What *did* happen to him? He disappeared. That's all we know. We've got to find out. And we'll be the first ones in Silver Creek to do it. I say all nine of us start out there tonight, after everyone's gone to sleep."

46

George looked drawn, as if it pained him to just think about defying his guardians. "But if Miss Ruth said all us kids were missing, that means we're not dead. Which means, if there are officials waiting to kill us, we could end up dead."

Kurt remembered the gunshot he'd heard earlier that day at the fence. The sheriff must be wondering what happened to him by now. He hadn't ridden his way around the fence as the sheriff had told him. Sheriff Dan seemed like the type who'd get insanely angry for defying him.

Kurt dismissed his fears. "We can't let that stop us. If a five-year-old can do it, so can we. Let's meet with the whole gang right before supper tonight, while the grown-ups are busy. Are you with me, George?"

George remained deep in thought for awhile, then a subtle grin lightened up his face. The two boys shook hands.

7.

When the sun was about halfway down the western sky, Kurt and George rounded up the rest of the kids and met with them in the open desert area just beyond the buildings. They set up the root beer bottles and took turns tossing pebbles at them, keeping their conspiracy to a whisper.

"Remember at dinner," said Kurt, "any extra food for the trip you can get your hands on, we'll wrap it and put it in our saddle bags, which we'll keep hidden under the table."

"How long will it take us to get there?" Haley Dawn asked.

"I don't know," said Kurt. "We should pack as much food as we can that won't spoil, at least a few days worth."

Some of them had stopped playing and looked at him, as if they might change their minds about going.

Just then, Kurt heard a voice call from far off. "I was wondering what happened to you? Skipping out on your job today, boy?"

Kurt turned and saw the sheriff on his horse. He didn't know how to answer. He didn't want to tell the sheriff about Miss Ruth's magical bird.

The children all froze as the sheriff walked his horse over to them. He dismounted gracefully, patted the horse's neck, and sauntered over to Kurt.

"Having a little fun and games for the kiddies?" he said, looking right into Kurt's face. "You know what happens to children who disobey the sheriff?"

Kurt felt as if he was sinking in his shoes.

"Whether you're aware of it or not, I have appointed myself to be your guardian. As guardian, I hereby dismiss your little entourage."

The children around Kurt seemed totally clueless that he was referring to them.

"Beat it!" he yelled. All the kids took off, leaving Kurt standing alone before the sheriff.

"Because you disobeyed me, your guardian, I have the right to discipline you. The punishment for failure to follow up on orders is ten lashes with the branch of an evergreen. In case you haven't seen one, they've got sharp needles as long as my little finger."

Kurt fought to maintain eye contact. He wasn't going to let this man intimidate him.

"And as sheriff, I have the right to keep you incarcerated—that means locked up—for as long as I want."

Kurt pulled out the photo from inside his shirt and gazed at it. "I bet you wouldn't have done this to Roy Sharp."

"Don't change the subject, boy."

Kurt turned the frame over and pointed out the sheriff's name. "Dan Calloway. That's you. You made the frame for this picture, didn't you?"

The sheriff still looked stern, but he didn't speak.

Kurt said nothing. Although he knew the picture was of Roy Robinson, he wasn't going to tell the sheriff.

"The glass is broken," the sheriff observed.

"Don't change the subject," said Kurt.

The sheriff thought a moment and chuckled a single syllable.

"You missed Roy Sharp," said Kurt. "I'll bet you were *his* guardian. And you made a frame for this picture so you or no one in Silver Creek would ever forget him."

He offered the picture to the sheriff. When the sheriff took it to examine it, there was a more thoughtful look on his face than before. Kurt's stomach churned, fearing that he might never get the picture back. He had to take it home with him, should he ever get home, to show Pa his dear son's picture he'd once left behind in Silver Creek.

"I sure do miss Roy," the sheriff said, immersed in his thoughts.

"I'll bet you do," Kurt said.

There was a long, heavy silence. The sheriff looked as if his mind was struggling to play back some old happy memories.

"I miss him," the sheriff repeated, shaking his head, "but by golly, if I could only remember him."

Kurt bit his lip. He struggled with his own feelings. He could tell that the sheriff once had a special connection with Roy, even though the picture was of Roy Robinson. Not for a second had the sheriff taken his eyes off the picture.

Then a loud clanging bell pealed from the village. The dinner bell.

The sheriff finally looked up and handed Kurt the picture. "Put this back where it belongs, boy." He turned away from Kurt, took the reins of his horse and walked it back toward town. "See you at dinner," he said.

Kurt watched him go, feeling like a weight had been taken off his shoulders. He took another look at the picture. "Thanks, Roy," he said. He swallowed a lump in his throat, thinking of the close call he'd just had. And for the first time since he arrived in Silver Creek, he felt himself sweating.

8.

At a dinner of fried beef and cabbage, Kurt had a horrible feeling in his stomach, as if he'd swallowed a beach ball. The kids' end of the long hall table was quiet. Communication consisted mostly of glances, reassuring each other that they were all in this together. From time to time, one of them would furtively wrap his or her biscuit or an ear of corn in a paper napkin and set it aside.

Kurt watched the sheriff eat. He was sitting across from Palmer and Joanne, who were doing most of the talking, and his eyes were mainly focused on his plate. He would nod occasionally to something they said. It seemed to Kurt that the sheriff had forgotten about their confrontation for the time. He wondered if the sheriff had really been Roy's guardian.

But Kurt was not Roy. And the sheriff had no right to appoint himself to be Kurt's guardian. Kurt didn't feel the need for a guardian.

After the plates had been empty for awhile, the adults' conversation and laughter grew louder, giving the children an opportunity to put their heads together and scheme.

"Let's start clearing the table," Kurt told them.

"Tiffany and I will bring the plates in the kitchen," said Haley Dawn.

"We'll help them," said Hoochie, indicating himself, Daniel, and Stephen.

"Good," said Kurt. "The rest of us will get the saddle bags ready in the kitchen so we can start loading up." But before the older boys headed off through the back door, Kurt went over to the grown-ups' table. "You all stay put. We're going to clear off the table for you."

"That's very thoughtful," one adult said.

"What a nice surprise," said another.

They all thanked the children and went on with their talking and laughing.

Kurt picked up handfuls of silverware. George and W.D. grabbed the platters of uneaten food. Eddie carefully stacked some of the plates and walked them into the kitchen. Kurt emptied the silverware in the sink and made room on the counter.

The younger children began parading into the kitchen with dirty dishes. Haley Dawn and Tiffany carried only a few at a time. Hoochie and Stephen wobbled in, each with an armful of teetering dinnerware.

"Take your time, guys," George told them. "There's no rush."

"We've got to go to the stable to get the saddlebags," said Kurt. "We'll be back in a few minutes."

Just then came a terribly loud crash that shook everyone's nerves. Adult voices started fussing. When Kurt burst into the dining hall, he saw Daniel in tears as Joanne and Patsy helped him pick up the pieces of broken plates and cups. They were saying to him, "Why don't you let us take care of the dishes?"

Some of the other grown-ups were beginning to get up when Kurt grabbed W.D. by the arm and pulled him out to the dining hall.

"Wait!" Kurt said to the crowd. "We were just about to start the entertainment part of our evening. W.D. here is going to play some music for us. Right, W.D.?"

The adults resumed sitting and expressed their pleasure by applauding.

W.D. looked put off, not his usual grinning self. He took a few seconds to compose himself, and then started in on a tune. At first it sounded like "Red River Valley", then it segued into "Get Along, Little Dogies."

The adults, so caught up in the entertainment, paid no attention to the rest of the children.

Kurt stepped away from the table, and goaded the younger kids to continue clearing the table. "Just don't take too much at one time," he told Daniel.

George and Eddie looked just as entranced as the adults.

"That son of a dhole," said George.

"You guys need to get the saddle bags from the stable," Kurt whispered to them. "Move it."

"We're moving," said Eddie. Their feet were heading toward the kitchen, but their faces stayed glued on W.D. until they left the room.

The younger kids race-walked in and out of the kitchen with the dishes and food scraps. Haley Dawn brushed the crumbs off the table. Hoochie poured all the various unused beverages into a jug, creating a sickening brownish-purple mixture.

When W.D. finished his medley, the adults cheered him. His cheeks were red, and he looked as

54

if he were out of breath. Kurt hurried over to him and patted his shoulder. "Do just a couple more," he whispered in W.D.'s ear. "We've got to stall them at least a few more minutes."

W.D. glared at him, as if he were considering putting his hands around Kurt's neck to strangle him.

"We're not quite finished, folks," Kurt announced. He stepped aside and everyone waited patiently as W.D. relaxed a bit and composed himself.

At first, Kurt thought W.D. wasn't going to do anything. But then he began to whistle "The Star Spangled Banner". He piped out one bar and stopped. Everyone sat in silence, waiting for him to continue. He repeated the same bar, and glared at Kurt.

Kurt was not going to let W.D. embarrass him. Somehow he found the nerve to open his mouth and sing, "Oh, say, can you seeee by the dawn's early light..." The adults all rose in respect of the National Anthem.

W.D. began to whistle a slightly lower harmony, making it harder for Kurt to find his pitch.

Kurt summoned all those hours he'd spent with Ma and Pa on Sunday mornings in church, singing those hymns. Where he'd been used to other voices drowning out his own, his voice was now out there alone. Only a soft murmur from the adults accompanied him.

"...O'er the la-and of the freeee and the home of the braaaave?"

The whole table burst into rapturous applause. They made a sensation of the two boys, tousling their hair and slapping their backs. Kurt held out his hand to W.D.

"Good work, W.D.," he said.

W.D.'s tired mouth twisted into a humble smile as he shook hands with his new friend.

The rest of the kids were standing at the door to the kitchen, clapping and cheering their approval. Eddie made a sign to Kurt to approach. Kurt hurried over as the adults began pushing in their chairs.

"The saddle bags are all packed and hidden inside the stable," Eddie told him. "The horses won't get at them."

"You guys work fast," said Kurt.

"And you guys weren't too shabby either," said George. He put his hand on W.D.'s shoulder. "I'm sorry I got mad at you before, pal. You may be a little nuts, but you always come through for your friends."

W.D. gave George a friendly shove.

9.

Everyone said their good-nights, but Kurt stayed to help Patsy finish cleaning up. He took the photo from his shirt so he could work more easily. Patsy was removing some food from the freezer to thaw overnight, when she stopped to pick up the picture.

"You got this from Palmer?" she asked.

"That's Roy Robinson," said Kurt. "My grandfather's son. He disappeared a long time ago, when he was only five."

Patsy leaned against the counter and gazed at the picture. "Funny how he looks so much like my little Roy."

"Roy Sharp?" Kurt asked, realizing that Patsy had the same last name.

"Mm-hmm. Did you hear how he first came to us?"

"Palmer said he rode into town on a donkey."

Patsy smiled. "I've seen that donkey around now and then. Usually it's on the other side of the fence. One time while I was mending a spot in the fence a windstorm had damaged, I swear I saw that donkey vanish into thin air. One minute it was there, looking around like it was hoping to find Roy. The next minute, he was gone." She snapped her fingers. "Shadow was its name. And it lived up to that name all right, always following Roy around like he was some special charm. He *was* some special charm." She smiled, but her eyes appeared wet.

Kurt started to feel awkward. He hated it when Ma cried, which she seldom did, since she hardly ever got upset. When Ma did cry, Kurt knew something was truly wrong, so wrong he felt a need to run off to save himself from crying. He fought that urge this time. He was older now.

He felt bad for Patsy, but what he really wanted at that moment was a shower or a bath. He hadn't bathed in the past two days, and he was starting to feel grubby.

"Were you his guardian?" he asked.

"Mostly. We all took turns caring for him, because he was the only child in Silver Creek. But back then we didn't have strict guardianship until the rest of the kids started coming. They came from what seemed like out of nowhere, and Palmer and Joanne put them all up in the hotel. They were so crazy and rowdy, we had to do something. That's when Dan decided to put each child in the care of an adult. From that point on, I became Roy's guardian."

She looked at Kurt. "You look tired. Would you like to spend the night? I've got Roy's old room."

Kurt was grateful for the invitation.

The house was set up similar to Miss Ruth's, only Patsy wasn't into bright colors or animals. There was a couch against one wall and sturdy chairs surrounding a low wooden table.

Patsy encouraged him to check out Roy's bedroom. There was a single small bed, much like the type in the hotel. The straw in the mattress felt firm and fresh, like it hadn't been used in years.

Wooden toys—a wagon, a horse, a donkey—were displayed on a chest of drawers. Kurt tugged open one of the drawers and pulled out one of Roy's old shirts. He unfolded it and held it up. It was a faded yellow and had a pattern of green diamond shapes all over it. It seemed like something Ma and Pa's Roy would have worn.

Kurt pulled all the shirts and trousers from the drawers to examine them. He unfolded one made of a soft, tough material, like chamois cloth. Another looked like a quilt, patches of blue and brown sewn together. There was a leather vest with long fringes, and a red and white bandana.

In the closet were one pair of children's cowboy boots and a pair of white and blue sneakers. Sneakers? he thought. How would a little boy from the Old West get sneakers?

On the closet floor was one shirt that was different from all the others—a white t-shirt with the words "Robinson's Old West" in faded red lettering.

"I've been looking all over for that," Patsy said, startling Kurt as she entered the room. "That's the shirt he was wearing when he first rode into town."

"I know this place," Kurt said in amazement. "My grandfather's last name is Robinson. Before I was adopted, he owned a park called Robinson's Old West. Roy was last seen in that park, and he must have been wearing this shirt."

"But I'm not talking about Roy Robinson," said Patsy. "I'm talking about Roy Sharp."

What Kurt had suspected, he finally realized to be very, very possible. He smiled at the thought of it. "Don't you see?" he said to Patsy. "They're the same person. Roy Sharp *is* Roy Robinson!"

Patsy stared at him for a moment and then burst out laughing. "What are you talking about? How could someone be two people at once?"

Kurt shook his head. "Not at once. Somehow Roy Robinson vanished and ended up here in Silver Creek. And when he rode into town on a donkey, wearing this shirt.... Did he tell you his name was Roy Robinson?"

Patsy frowned. "I can't remember," she said.

"Try," Kurt told her. "Please try."

"I can't!" she cried. Her face was twisted in frustration as she left the room.

Kurt sat back down on the bed and sighed. That did it for him. Holding on to all these possessions wouldn't help Patsy remember any more than she could. Or maybe she just didn't want to.

Ma and Pa would be delighted to discover some of Roy's old things. It would be the best present he could ever give them. It would feel to them like Roy was back in their lives. But first, Kurt wanted to be back in their lives.

Kurt wasn't certain that he'd ever find his way back to Ohio. But if he did, he sure wasn't going to show up empty-handed.

10.

Kurt was wide awake, even though the hour was very late. Seeing Patsy so upset about Roy Sharp possibly having a connection with Roy Robinson made him upset, too. What was it with these grown-ups? All Kurt wanted to know was the truth. The truth about how they all got here. The truth about Roy Sharp. The truth about himself being dead, missing, or neither. Why did they all have such a hard time with the truth?

Maybe they just didn't know. Perhaps Miss Ruth had been right all along, that he was sent to Silver Creek to tell them why they were here.

That's not my job, he thought as he lay awake on the crinkly bed. As if it were his responsibility to help all the adults in town.

I'm taking these kids with me, he told himself. I'm kind of like their leader, and hopefully we'll all find our way out of Silver Creek together.

Wherever this journey would take them, whatever it held in store for them, it was forbidden by the adults. That only made the prospect of getting to the Edge all the more exciting for Kurt. It filled him with energy.

He got to his feet. He picked up Roy's old t-shirt and sneakers. He tied the laces of the sneakers together to make them easier to carry and hung them around his neck. He rolled the t-shirt into a tight ball and stuffed it in his pants pocket. The other things belonged to Roy Sharp, the Roy who

61

Patsy knew and loved. Kurt didn't want to take that away from her.

The photo! He never saw where Patsy had put it.

He crept through the house in the dark, searching for the silver-framed picture. He scanned the living room slowly, stopping at the low table, the writing desk, and the kitchen counter, but found nothing. There were no electric lights in the house. Thinking Patsy must have candles somewhere, he slid open some kitchen drawers, but found none.

Her bedroom, he thought. It was possible she had put the picture on her nightstand so that Roy's smiling face was the last she saw before falling off to sleep. That's where Ma kept the pictures of her own family.

The door to Patsy's bedroom was leaning shut. When Kurt carefully pushed it open, it groaned a little. The light from the moonlit sky illuminated her room in a soft glow. He heard no movement in the room, not even a sound of breathing. It seemed as if she might not be there at all. Either that, or she was just a very sound sleeper.

Just as he suspected, there was the silver frame, standing on her bedside table. He padded across the floor, and lifted up the frame. Roy's face was shadowed behind the glass, which was now intact. Patsy must have replaced it, he thought.

He could just make out the outline of her slumbering body on the bed. Her back was toward him. Standing still, he could see the middle part of her body gently rising and falling with her breath. She would miss this picture, Kurt thought. But it belonged to Pa. Kurt had to get it back to him.

62

Ma and Pa used to tell Kurt over and over again about how they took him into their home when he was lost. Although he couldn't remember the events happening to him, it was because his grandparents had told him the story countless times. Yet, a part of him was always awakened whenever they told him that story. Deep inside him, there was a memory, more like a feeling, of being found and taken to a loving place. A feeling he had no words for. The feeling seemed to always come from his chest, about where his heart was. Perhaps that was the same feeling the adults had when they remembered Roy. If only they had told his story more often, perhaps they would not have so much unhappiness inside them.

Kurt gave the picture one last glance before tucking it away in his shirt. He placed it on the side of his shirt closest to his heart.

So long, Patsy, he said in his mind. Maybe I'll find Roy for you. If I do, I'll tell him you miss him and want him back.

He stepped as quietly out of the room as he came, made his way through the house, and closed the front door behind him.

The air was comfortable and cool. The only sound was the breeze sweeping across the desert, rustling the small neighboring trees. Kurt walked around the back of the houses and down a short path. When he reached George's house he knocked on the closed shutter of his bedroom window.

It opened. George stuck his face out. "I'll go round up W.D., Eddie, and the two girls," he said to Kurt. "You get the others."

Kurt wound his way along the path, trying not to wake anyone. He found Hoochie's house and knocked on his bedroom shutter, then did the same for Stephen, and finally Daniel.

Kurt waited inside the stable, and in two minutes, they were all assembled. Kurt counted eight faces. Some looked eager, some anxious. All looked tired and grimy.

"Let's at least get past the fence before we camp out," said Kurt.

"We should double up on the horses," said George.

"Yeah," said Haley Dawn. "That way if someone gets lost, they'll have a friend with them."

Tiffany gave her an anxious smile.

"I don't know," said Eddie. "I think we should each take one. Because when the grown-ups find out we're gone, it will be harder for them to go look for us. Especially if there are fewer horses."

George shook his head. "They wouldn't all come looking for us. Mostly the sheriff and Palmer, and Dashiel and the other guys."

The thought of the sheriff coming after them sent a chill down Kurt's back. "You're both right. But I think George's idea is better. We can't afford to lose anyone."

"But there's nine of us," said Stephen. "Hoochie and Daniel and me can ride together on Magic Thunder."

"No, that's too many," said George. "One of us will have to ride alone."

"I'll go with Eddie," said Daniel.

"I'll ride alone," said Kurt.

"That leaves me and old Happy Tunes here," said George. He and W.D. gave each other a high ten.

The children saddled up their favorite horses. Kurt noticed a donkey with short pointed ears. Its gray fur was soft, and its eyes had been closed.

"Is this Shadow?" Kurt asked.

"I don't know," said Haley Dawn. "I've never seen it before."

"You're going to ride a donkey?" said Daniel.

"Aren't you afraid you'll break him?" said Hoochie. The three youngest boys fell over one another in laughter.

"Not any faster than I'll break your jaw bones," said Kurt. "Now let's get out of here before someone hears us. You know the way to get us on the other side of the fence?" he asked George.

"There's a gate," said George. "Just follow us."

They mounted their beasts and left the village with only the sounds of hooves padding the dirt path. The houses remained dark and still, showing no evidence that the band of travelers had disturbed anyone's sleep.

When they reached the open desert, Kurt rode just behind George and W.D. He was glad someone besides him had ridden the fence. The donkey made smooth strides, its head bowing slightly.

Kurt could barely make out the outline of the mountains against the gray sky. He thought of those mountains as the door to possibilities. He knew not what they would find. They might find danger, or perhaps answers to some of their deepest questions. They might find nothing but more desert, with another village like Silver Creek, cut off from the rest of the world.

Kurt felt the cool silver frame pressing against his chest, near his heart. "Take us there, Roy," he said. "Help us to find what we're looking for."

The kids all knew exactly where the gate was, since they had all ridden fence for the sheriff many times.

"What's the point in checking the fence?" Kurt asked, as W.D. dismounted to unhook the gate.

"Wild animals," said George. "Dholes mostly, I guess. No one's ever seen any."

"Ever heard any gunshots?"

"No," said George, looking curiously at Kurt. "Have you?"

"When I came out here to ride fence with the sheriff. I was sore from riding the horse, so I rested awhile. That's when I saw Miss Ruth's pet bird sitting on the fence post. Not long after that, I heard a gunshot like it was real close. Just about scared the hairs off my arms."

Kurt looked around, and saw the mouths of some of the tired faces parted open in fright.

"I could have imagined it," Kurt said, sorry that he'd scared them. "I'm sure it was something else. You know what they say about being in desert for awhile. Sometimes your mind starts playing tricks on you." He laughed to get them to do the same, but they all just looked at one another.

"Gate's open!" Kurt announced, as W.D. stood back, holding the door like a royal sentry.

Once they passed through the gate, W.D. rewired it shut, and they all began to dismount and settle in for the night.

Using his saddlebag for a pillow, even with the rolled t-shirt on top of it, Kurt found it impossible to

66

sleep. The ground was as hard and dry as a piece of stale cake. The rest of the kids snored and grunted away the hours like pigs on a bed of hay. No gunshots were fired that night.

11.

Just as the sun was coming up for the second full day he'd been in Silver Creek, Kurt reached in his saddlebag and began munching on biscuits. He devoured them in a matter of minutes. He didn't realize how little he'd eaten the morning before. Ma always served him huge portions. Just recently, a normal breakfast for him consisted of six French toast or homemade blueberry pancakes, whereas a year ago, three would have filled him.

Once the whole troop was roused and fed, they continued on their journey. They traveled for miles, passing one giant stalk of cactus after another. Silver Creek soon became a dot under the western horizon. Observing the midmorning sun, Kurt figured they'd covered about twenty miles. The mountains before them were looming larger and higher than ever.

They were all so excited at the prospect of reaching the Edge that, hungry as they were, they never bothered to stop for snacks. By the time the sun was directly overhead, they saw nothing but mountain staring right in their faces.

"We're here!" Hoochie shouted. "We made it!"

They all slid off their mounts and hobbled, sore-bottomed, to the rocky face of a mountain and lay their hands on it.

The rock generated a warm heat into Kurt's hands, a heat that traveled up his arms, and throughout his body. He took his hands away from the rock for a moment. The sensation remained in his body. Again, he pressed his hands upon the rock, which sent warm heat all the way down his body into his toes, rising up to his head.

"Do you feel heat coming from the rock?" Eddie asked from down the line.

Everyone did. They all copied Kurt, taking their hands away to feel the warmth staying with them, then placing their hands back on the rock to receive more. In fact, the time when they felt the warmth most intensely was when they were all pressing their hands against the rock at the same time.

They all remained motionless for several minutes, after which Kurt began to feel a different sensation. Along with the warm heat, there was a soft vibration, such as he'd never felt before, that stimulated his hands. He felt the vibration pass quickly over his entire body, energizing him.

"You feel that?" someone said.

"Sssh," came the answer.

The vibration quickened, ever softly. Kurt closed his eyes and concentrated on the vibration as it brought out of his brain a picture.

At first, all he could see in his mind's eye were shadows, images of people walking slowly past him in all directions. Some of the people were as tall as giants, and some were just as tall as he.

The images became sharper and more colorful. There was a big wheel in the sky, and a mountain that screamed.

He felt very small in this place. Small and alone. Someone was missing. Someone had been there and had left him. There was a puddle of ice cream at his feet, and a sugar cone in his hand. And Kurt felt afraid, very afraid. He started to sob.

"Hey, pal! What's wrong?"

Kurt felt as if he'd just been awakened from a dream. That entire scene had disappeared, but the scared, lonely feeling stayed with him. His friends were all standing around him—George and W.D., Haley Dawn and Tiffany, and the rest of the kids. They were like breathing statues.

"Kurt, what happened?" George asked.

The vision he had of the people, and holding an ice cream cone, had been erased from his memory. All he saw now were the mountains at his side, and the vast expanse of desert. He remembered crossing it.

"Something," Kurt said, his mouth half-opened. "Something..."

"I felt a buzzing feeling go through me," said Haley Dawn.

"We all felt it," Hoochie said on behalf of his trio. "I never knew a mountain could do that."

"Let's try a different one," said Daniel. The five youngest kids all took off, laughing. They placed their hands on the mountain and stood as still as they could.

"Are you really okay, pal?" George asked.

"You sounded like you were crying," said Eddie.

"I can't remember what I saw," Kurt said. "It was like being in a dream, and I just remember feeling lonely and scared. And small."

"I didn't have any dream," said George. He looked at W.D. and Eddie. "What about you guys?"

W.D. shook his head.

"I think I can remember something," said Eddie. "I felt like I was up really high, and there was something under me, like wings."

"Anything else?" George asked.

Eddie looked disappointed. "No, not really."

The young ones were running toward them at full speed. But Kurt counted only four kids, and their faces were full of terror.

"Kurt!" Hoochie cried. "We can't find Daniel. I think he's gone!"

"How could he be gone?" said Kurt. "There's nowhere to hide around here."

"Daniel!" George hollered. His voice echoed off the mountains.

Kurt and Eddie joined in until all three of their voices made a resounding chorus. "Dan-iel-iel-iel-iel-iel! Dan-iel-iel-iel-iel-iel!"

When the echo died down, there was only the sound of tears. Hoochie was bawling his eyes out. "It wasn't my fault. He was right next to me the whole time we were touching the mountain."

"I felt something around me," said Tiffany. "Like a black cloud, and it felt like it was going to pull me in. Then I opened my eyes."

"You felt this while you were touching the mountain?" Kurt asked.

Tiffany nodded, biting her lip.

"I had the same kind of feeling," said Hoochie.

"So did I," said Stephen.

"Me too," said Haley Dawn.

"I knew we shouldn't have come out here," said George. "This place is too creepy."

Just then, they heard a gunshot go off and echo against the mountains. Though not quite as loud as the one Kurt had heard by the fence, it still gripped him with fear. It was hard to pinpoint where it had come from. It could have come from anywhere. They all froze, staring at one another in horror.

"Was that what I thought it was?" Eddie asked.

71

"I hope it's not Daniel," Hoochie sobbed. "What if the officials got him? What if he's dead?"

Another gunshot rocked the air. Only this one sounded as if it were only yards away. The horses and the donkey scattered, running off in different directions. The eight children scrambled to the ground and formed a tight circle.

12.

They watched their horses gallop across the desert plains. Strapped to the horses' backs were the saddlebags holding the troop's food supply. Gone. Soon all that was visible were the clouds of dust their hooves left in their wake.

The Eight were packed together like vagabonds huddled close to a fire. Haley Dawn's teeth chattered as if she were cold.

Kurt's stomach rumbled. "We've got to find a way to get past the Edge," he said. "Maybe our best choice is to just climb this mountain."

"But we can't go without Daniel," said Eddie. "He's one of us."

"Maybe he's already over there," said Stephen. "We don't even know where the Edge is. Do we?"

Everyone looked at Kurt as if he had the answer. He knew it was his fault he got them into this mess. He had earned their confidence, and now he felt responsible for getting them all past the Edge.

"Mr. Jackson lives around here somewhere," said Kurt. "Dashiel told me he lives just on the other side of the Edge. Think we should try to find him?"

"How would we do that?" George asked. "These mountains go on for miles all the way around. He could live anywhere."

"Maybe we should just get over the mountains first," said Kurt. "At least we'll be safer there."

"But then if Daniel's still on this side of the Edge, he'll never find us," said Hoochie.

It was quiet for awhile as eight heads tried to work out a solution.

And then, out of the stillness, from W.D.'s rounded lips came a warm, comforting whistle. It was like an airy chant that settled their brains and calmed their fears.

W.D. got to his feet and began walking alongside the mountains. Everyone rose and followed behind him. As he led the troop, he kept whistling. The tune grew into a bright, cheerful melody that put a bounce in their steps.

The others joined in, some more boldly than others. Kurt was one of the bold ones. From time to time W.D. turned and grinned his way. George elbowed Kurt as they walked and whispered to him, "Can't you carry a tune, man?"

"You heard me sing the other night," said Kurt, taking a bit of offense. "I'm just not a great whistler."

"I think you're good," said Haley Dawn. "You can whistle a lot louder than me."

Kurt was flattered. He felt his face get a little hot. "Thanks, Haley Dawn," he said.

They kept following W.D., who whistled the whole time he walked, stopping only to change tunes. Together they marched like a small desert regiment. Knowing that another gunshot could possibly take one of them, their lives were on the line. They had nothing left but themselves and their confidence that hope was within reach.

As they marched, those following the Whistler took a break from their own whistling to call out their friend's name. "Dan-iel!"

74

The mountains echoed their voices back and forth, creating a chorus.

"Dan-iel-iel-iel-iel-iel!"

The hours groaned by, marked by their shoe prints in the hardened sand. Their voices strained, their calls had long ceased. The Whistler had grown weary, his head hanging.

Kurt put his hand on W.D.'s shoulder. "You're really something, W.D. Just look how far you've gotten us."

They all turned around and looked at where they'd been. But the mountains from their new location looked no different from the ones they had their eyes focused on for the past few hours.

"It looks like we haven't gone anywhere," said George. "Like we've ended up where we started."

"I can't walk anymore," said Tiffany, her legs buckling like noodles.

"We've been walking all day," said Eddie. "And I'm hungry."

Kurt could tell by the position of the sun that it was late afternoon. Soon, it would be hidden behind the jagged horizon. "Why don't we sit down and rest," he said.

They stretched out on the dusty ground at the base of the mountain. To Kurt, even the hard rock beneath his head felt like a soft pillow.

His brain was a noisy racket, echoing their whistled tunes and their calls for Daniel. He hated to think Daniel was dead, taken down by an official with a gun.

13.

The breeze picked up as the sun began its descent behind the mountains. And with that breeze, Kurt caught a familiar scent. A fabulous scent. He sat up and sniffed the air. It was definitely food. Food that would feed his hungry troops.

He got up and followed the scent to a nearby cave, not far from where they had camped for the evening.

When he peered inside, he saw that it was really a tunnel. He stepped inside. On the other side of the tunnel was a house—a small white house with red shutters, and a sign outside in the shape of a sunflower, on which was written the name Jackson. If this was the Mr. Jackson Dashiel had told him about, then this must be the other side of the Edge, he thought.

It was quite the opposite of Silver Creek. There was bright green grass all around and flowers blooming by the acres. The sun cast a yellow glow over the distant rolling hills. He thought he heard the sound of gently running water from far off. The Jackson house seemed to be the only house around.

Kurt had an urge to break forward and run onto the open green pasture. The smell of food he had detected before was coming from the Jackson house, and he recognized it for what it was. Chocolate chip cornbread.

But it was impossible. It had to be. As far as he knew, no one baked chocolate chip cornbread but his Ma.

He put one foot out onto the green grass, and sensing there was no danger, he strolled across the pasture and onto the stone walkway that led to the little house.

He knocked on the wooden door. An elderly black man, at least he looked elderly to Kurt, answered. He was smaller than Dashiel, and wore a long multicolored buttoned shirt and trousers.

"My goodness," he said as he gazed at Kurt. He put his hand on his chest. "I do believe it's Roy Sharp, come back after all these years."

"No, sir. My name is Kurt Van Loon, from Ohio. Are you Mr. Jackson?"

The man looked both puzzled and bewildered. "Yes. Earl Jackson."

Kurt hesitated. He hated to come right out and ask a stranger for something to eat. But this man seemed warm and kind, and Kurt was so hungry, he thought he'd pass out.

"Would you have something for me to eat, sir? I'm very hungry." He took a deep whiff of the aroma wafting from inside the house. "Something sure smells good. Is it chocolate chip cornbread?"

Mr. Jackson smiled. "Why, yes. It was Roy Sharp's favorite. I just happened to be making some. Won't you come in?"

He held the door wide as Kurt stepped inside the tiny house. His eyes feasted on plates and bowls made of copper and silver, hanging on racks, and some on shelves.

"The sheriff in Silver Creek has a plate like that," Kurt said. "So does Miss Ruth."

"Yes, I know. I made them," said Mr. Jackson. "Come sit down."

Kurt sat at the blue table by the window. Bathed in the late afternoon sun, it felt like his grandmother's kitchen. There were jars of spices on a rack, and blue and white checkered dishtowels about the room.

Mr. Jackson set a plate of cubed cornbread on the table. "These came from the oven just a few minutes ago. Help yourself."

The moment Kurt sank his teeth into the moist cornbread, a cozy feeling came over him. He had the feeling of being back at home, warm and dry inside on a cold rainy day, with a plate of chocolate chip cornbread in front of him.

Kurt ate three huge hunks and washed them down with milk. He closed his eyes and eased himself downward in his chair. "Now that was good!" he said.

"Funny thing," said Mr. Jackson. "It was exactly what Roy Sharp asked me for when he stopped by my house years ago. I hadn't made this cornbread in years. Once in a while, I make it, hoping I'll see Roy again. Whenever I smell it baking, I can just picture Roy, riding by on that donkey."

"Dashiel back in Silver Creek said you saw Roy disappear into thin air."

"That he did. Come with me, and I'll show you."

Kurt followed Mr. Jackson out to the front walk. Mr. Jackson pointed to the open area of pasture. "Right about there is where he vanished. He told me he had a lot of fun in Silver Creek, but that he missed his mommy and daddy something fierce. He asked me if I knew where Robinson's Old West was." He looked at Kurt, puzzled. "When he described it to me, I told the young boy I hadn't a clue."

"I know what Robinson's Old West was," said Kurt. "It used to be my grandfather's old theme park. He closed it right after his son Roy Robinson disappeared from the park."

Mr. Jackson looked puzzled. "Robinson?"

Kurt pulled the picture out of his shirt. "This is Roy Robinson."

Mr. Jackson took his half-glasses from his shirt pocket and put them on to examine the photo. "Son of a gun. All this time I thought this was Roy Sharp."

"I think they're the same person," said Kurt. "Patsy has a t-shirt that belonged to Roy that said 'Robinson's Old West' on it. She said it was the shirt he was wearing when he rode into Silver Creek. Although, nobody seemed to know how Roy got here. Do you?"

Mr. Jackson looked down in deep thought, then shook his head slowly. "Afraid I don't, Mr. Van Loon."

"Or George, or W.D., or any of the kids? How does someone get into Silver Creek anyway?" Kurt felt defeated. He looked pleadingly at Mr. Jackson.

The old man smiled sadly. "How does a body find his way to Silver Creek?" He shook his head again. "By accident, I suppose."

"Is that how you got here, Mr. Jackson? By accident?"

"Let's go for a walk, Mr. Van Loon." He patted Kurt's shoulder and guided him along a narrow path of rich, brown earth, along the mountains. He was quiet for awhile.

Kurt grew impatient for him to begin explaining.

"I remember my wife Ruby, sitting by my bedside. My doctor told me days before that I should spend my last living days at home. I passed away while my dear Ruby was holding my hand and singing to me. When I passed on, I thought for sure that beautiful light I saw meant I was going to meet my Creator. I had to say I was a bit disappointed when he landed me here."

The elderly man laughed. "I said, 'Lord, who are you kidding, putting me up in some poor little house?' Back then that little house we were in was just an old shack. But I fixed it up good, now didn't I?"

"It's a nice place," said Kurt. "So, you died and you just ended up here?"

"I was walking down what I suppose you might call a long hallway or a tunnel. And the end of it, the place I first found myself, was right there."

Kurt halted. "Right where?"

"You're standing on it now."

Kurt looked down at the ground around his feet. It looked like any other ordinary patch of rich, green grass. He gazed out over the flowery meadow that rolled on like an ocean.

"It's so perfect here," said Kurt. "Why are you the only one living on this side of the Edge, and everyone else is in Silver Creek?"

Mr. Jackson shrugged. "Folks make their own choices. They could live here if they wanted, I guess. I do my best to be a good neighbor. That's why I brought them those gifts."

Kurt could hear the sound of gurgling water in the distance. "Is that a creek I hear?"

"That's Silver Creek. It used to run right through those mountains. Mountains got so high, the creek couldn't flow past them anymore."

"How did the mountains get high?" Kurt asked.

Mr. Jackson began slowly. "Well, it all started when Dan Calloway first came to Silver Creek on that tall horse of his and asked me where he could find a place to stay. I showed him that building where he now lives, back in the village where you were. 'Course there was no village back then, just a little shack like mine. He became my apprentice for a while. Some of those copper pots you saw in my house were actually done by him."

"That explains how the sheriff made that picture frame!" Kurt said excitedly. "You showed him how to get the copper and silver from the creek bed."

"That's correct," Mr. Jackson answered. "But something in that man changed, turned dark and ugly. He became hateful. Wanted no more to do with me. Must have been because I had spoken to Roy Sharp before he disappeared. He didn't want anyone, especially the rest of the kids, to know about Roy escaping. Since then those mountains started growing. The creek stopped flowing past them, and that's why you have that there desert."

Kurt was amazed. One man's bitterness had turned a beautiful paradise into a hardscrabble desert.

"Now how about you?" Mr. Jackson asked. "How did you find your way to Silver Creek?"

"I passed out on top of a mountain back home. And when I woke up, I was in Silver Creek. Palmer says all the grown-ups in Silver Creek are dead. Since I'm thirteen, I guess that means I'm dead, too."

Mr. Jackson shook his head. "You most certainly are not dead, Mr. Van Loon. None of the kids in Silver Creek are dead. You can go back. You can all go back together if you want."

"But how? They can't even remember how they got here. How am I supposed to help them find their way back? The mountain that brought me here is gone."

Mr. Jackson placed a steadying hand on Kurt's shoulder. "You're making things much too difficult, Mr. Van Loon. It's all very simple."

"Then what do I have to do?"

"The answer is all in these here mountains. There's a power in them."

"I know. When we put our hands on them, I remembered a scene from when I was five. I was in an amusement park, and I felt lost and lonely, like someone had left me, and..."

"And what?" Mr. Jackson asked.

"I don't know, I stopped."

"You stopped? Why?"

"It was too painful. That, and Daniel had disappeared."

Kurt could feel the man's eyes burning holes right into his soul. "Go back, son, before another one of you disappears. Go back and put your hands on that mountain and make yourselves remember."

"But what about the officials? They could kill us. We heard gunshots not that long ago."

"Officials?" Mr. Jackson repeated, as if Kurt had spoken nonsense. "Gunshots? Son, there's nothing for you to be afraid of but your own fear."

14.

There was nothing more to say. Mr. Jackson sent Kurt away with a cloth sack of chocolate chip cornbread and a new sense of purpose.

The sun had now set fully behind the mountains, turning the sky pink and purple. Kurt felt his way through the tunnel that brought him back out to the desert side of the mountains. Only now when he looked around, he realized he was alone.

He began calling out for his companions, name by name. But all he heard was the sound of his own tired, raspy voice echoing faintly in the mountains.

He sat on the smooth surface at the foot of the mountain and watched the sky darken. The thought of all his friends vanishing into thin air chilled him.

"Please," he said aloud, burying his face in his hands. "They can't all be gone. Please tell me they can't all be gone." He was so tired, he didn't even know who he was speaking to.

Put your hands on the mountain, he kept hearing Mr. Jackson's voice say in his head.

I don't care about the mountain anymore, he told himself. He just wanted to find his friends. Perhaps they had all continued in their search for Daniel. But why would they leave me behind? Kurt wondered.

He sat motionless on the rock until long after the sky had grown completely dark.

Then he heard footsteps, at least four of them, approaching in the darkness. He listened to determine how close they would get. When they stopped, he heard a snort and a heavy sigh.

"George?" he asked, hoping that it wasn't an official with a shotgun. "Is it you and W.D.?"

The footsteps grew closer, only they sounded more like clop-clop. A man on a horse, he thought. Could it be the sheriff? He remembered what the sheriff had told him, that he would make Kurt's stay in Silver Creek very difficult.

It turned out to be an animal, which reached its nose out to sniff the bag in Kurt's hands.

Kurt recognized the donkey that he had ridden on his way out to the mountains. "Hey, boy!" he said to the animal. "I thought you were long gone."

The donkey kept nosing at the bag.

"All right, one piece," said Kurt. He broke off a small hunk of chocolate chip cornbread, and the donkey took it gently from Kurt's hand. Kurt stroked the fur on its neck. "How the heck did you find me? And where are all the others?"

He caught sight of something unusual dangling from the donkey's neck. It was Roy's sneakers, tied together at the laces.

Strange, Kurt thought. He clearly remembered stashing them in the saddlebag. Somebody must have found Shadow and put them there. Had to be one of the kids. Who else would have known about the sneakers? And if a grown-up back in Silver Creek had discovered them, they wouldn't have just draped them over the donkey's neck.

The donkey sniffed the sneakers and then licked Kurt's face. What was this creature doing? Kurt wondered. Was it making some sort of connection between Roy's sneakers and Kurt.

Kurt sniffed the sneakers. To him, they had no smell, as if they hadn't been worn in years. But perhaps the donkey could sense something that Kurt could not.

"Don't tell me you think I'm Roy Sharp, too?" he said to the animal. "Just because he rode out of Silver Creek on a donkey like you." As Kurt was petting the animal's fur, he thought of the story someone in Silver Creek had told him about Roy Sharp.

"Shadow?" Kurt said.

The animal licked Kurt's hand.

Kurt got to his feet and walked several steps away from the mountains. "Come here, Shadow!" he called.

To Kurt's amazement, the donkey turned and started walking in that slow dipping way of his right over to his master.

Kurt stroked the donkey's neck. "Son of a gun! You can't be the same donkey that Roy Sharp rode out of Silver Creek." Kurt laughed out loud. "That would make you an old donkey!"

He heard his laughter echo against the mountains, sounding as if it were laughing back at him. Quiet! he told himself. You want some crazy official to come shooting at you?

He faced Shadow and looked right into one of his big, brown eyes. "I promise to be real quiet, if you can take me to that mountain, the one that vibrated and gave me that weird dream. I'll even let you have more cornbread."

He put the sack of cornbread in the saddlebag. There was not enough room for the sneakers, so he hung them around his own neck and hoisted himself onto the donkey. The animal turned completely around and started walking, as if it knew exactly where to take Kurt.

The donkey's gait was slow, making gentle rocking and bouncing motions, which put Kurt at ease. He hadn't realized how tired he had been until now. Closing his eyes, he held the reins firmly. The sneakers thumped softly against his chest in a regular rhythm.

He remembered what Mr. Jackson had told him. *Put your hands on the mountain, and make yourselves remember.*

The memory of himself alone, holding that ice cream cone, had been painful. The thought of enduring more pain did not thrill him. But he had convinced himself that it might be his only way back to his family.

"I'm going to the mountain," Kurt mumbled as he fell into a light sleep. "I'm going to make myself remember."

15.

The next thing Kurt knew, he was awakened by the donkey's sudden stop. He had arrived at a mountain. It didn't look any different from the other mountains in the ridge.

He dismounted and fed a piece of cornbread to Shadow. He stepped up to the mountain and took a few deep breaths. He looked back at the donkey. "Do I really have to do this, boy?"

The donkey brayed softly.

Kurt placed the palms of his hands on the surface of the mountain. He closed his eyes and waited. Still half asleep from the ride, he was able to stay relaxed.

First came the warm heat, oozing into his hands, then up his arms and throughout his whole body. Kurt relaxed even more.

Next came the vibration, pulsating softly, like a kitten's heartbeat. It tickled his palms at first, but then he grew accustomed to it, and soon his entire body felt like it was vibrating.

A picture began to form in his mind.

Giants walking past him...a big wheel in the sky... a screaming mountain ... a puddle of ice cream at his feet. He was holding a sugar cone.

He felt the fear coming on. Someone was missing. Knowing this intensified his fear and loneliness. Kurt was five years old again.

Five-year-old Kurt felt a sob coming up. He stifled it, and forced himself to look more closely at the images around him. The giants were only grown-ups, and they were smiling and walking with their children. The big wheel in the sky was a Ferris wheel. And the screaming mountain was no more than a roller coaster, with riders screaming with delight.

Just then he caught sight of something fluttering to the ground. He picked it up. It was in the shape of a rectangle, and it had a blue border and big black letters on it. Four of them—K-U-R-T. Looking around, he saw that other little kids like him had signs like these stuck to their shirts. The little kids were walking in big groups, holding hands, with a grown-up leading them.

A gray-haired lady came, carrying an ice cream cone. She smiled as she took the empty cone out of Kurt's sticky hand and replaced it with a new one. "Here you are, sweetheart," the lady said. "All better."

The new ice cream cone tasted good.

"Oh, so your name is Kurt?" the lady asked.

Kurt looked up in surprise. The name didn't sound quite right. Why?

The lady bent down so she was eye level with him. She gently took the name tag from Kurt's hand and showed it to him. "Is that your name, honey?" she asked.

Kurt couldn't think of his real name. He couldn't even remember where he'd been just five minutes before. He only remembered himself crying because he felt very alone.

"Is your mommy here with you?"

Kurt tried to picture his mother, but he couldn't. He looked around. None of the ladies walking by looked familiar. He shook his head.

"Were you with your teacher?"

He shook his head.

"Let's go talk to somebody," the lady said, taking his hand. She brought him to a little house that had a sign with the letters "O-F-F-I-C-E".

There were more grown-ups inside. They looked like police officers. A lady and a man. They checked lists, called people on the telephone, and shook their heads. They were sorry. No one named Kurt had been missing. The gray-haired lady gave the police officers her name and telephone number.

"Aberdine Robinson," she had said.

For some reason, the sound of that name warmed him inside. He felt less afraid. In fact, his fear had all melted away like that ice cream on the ground.

"Do you live in a big house?" he asked her when they got back outside.

"It's pretty big, I would say," the lady answered. She was quiet for awhile, as if she were thinking.

They walked slowly. Kurt licked his ice cream.

She stopped and looked at him. "Would you like to see it?" she asked.

A smile tickled Kurt's face. There was something about this lady that felt right. He wanted to know more about her. He nodded his head vigorously.

The scene ended like a movie reel. Kurt was thirteen again. His eyes shot open. He slowly withdrew his hands from the smooth surface of the mountain. The vibration and warmth had escaped him, although some of it stayed with him. He looked around and saw Shadow, standing patiently.

Kurt mulled over his experience. He remembered it all now. The gray-haired lady was his Ma and she had taken him home with her. Now he knew how he got his name. The stories his grandparents had told him now had meaning. They became more than stories. They were part of Kurt.

He was very tired now. He found a comfortable spot on the sandy ground, and used the saddlebag for a pillow. After not sleeping well the previous night, he hoped that sleep would come quickly this time.

It did. His mind quiet, and the whirring desert wind calming him, he soon drifted off to sleep. He dreamed of being back in Ma and Pa's house, watching TV or reading one of the Pa's books on the Old West. He dreamed of sitting on the porch with them, eating blueberry strudel.

But he was soon awakened from his peaceful sleep by the sound of howling. He couldn't tell if there were many howls, or just the same one echoing against the mountains. It was hard for him to judge the distance, but the very first howl seemed quite close. Shadow stirred from his sleep and lifted his head.

Were they the dholes the kids had told him about? Or maybe they were coyotes scavenging for food. What was there for them to eat in this place anyway? There didn't seem to be many small animals around. Kurt hadn't recalled seeing one single rat, jackrabbit, or lizard. Not that a coyote would eat a lizard, would it?

Just then he heard Shadow gallop off. What now? he wondered as he sat up.

He heard panting and the sound of paws scraping the dry ground. In the moonlight the animals looked dark red, the color of blood, and their coats thick and heavy. They were too big and hairy to be coyotes. Their yellow eyes glinted in the darkness like twelve round marbles.

Kurt remained very still as one of the dog-beasts sat down. The others looked off in other directions as if guarding prey, or potential prey they had found.

Kurt shuddered visibly. They turned their attention to him and one started to growl lightly as if he were giving Kurt a message, as if they could read his thoughts and feelings.

They know I'm scared, Kurt thought. The growling increased like fire.

Kurt reached into his bag and tossed a hunk of chocolate chip cornbread in their direction. They dove after it, with several snarling at one another. In seconds, the scuffle was over and they were all staring at him again. Kurt thought he saw the hair on their backs stand up.

He tossed them another piece. And the snarling and the yipping intensified. He only had so much cornbread in his bag. The way they were gobbling it up, there wouldn't be enough to satisfy all of them. He kept tossing out small morsels at longer and longer intervals. And the longer they waited, the closer they got until they were no more than a few steps away.

He threw out his last piece, which disappeared into a hungry mouth before it hit the ground. Then it was just him and the pack of hungry animals.

Just then he heard a whistle coming from far off. It sounded like W.D., whistling a tune that pierced the night, making the darkness feel less dark and threatening.

The dogs all turned their heads, their ears raised.

They weren't going to go after W.D., were they? Kurt wondered.

The song filled the night air, the wind carrying it closer. It was a sweet song, much like the ones Kurt and Ma sang in church.

Then one of the dogs lay down, and put his head on his paws. One by one, the others followed, and together they made a collective whimpering sound.

WD was coming out of the darkness, waving to Kurt. He kept on whistling.

16.

When the whistling stopped, W.D. broke into a grin and ran at full speed toward Kurt.

"Where have you been?" said Kurt. "Did you think I was lost?"

W.D. nodded.

"I was hungry," Kurt explained. "I smelled chocolate chip cornbread, and I followed it to Mr. Jackson's house. He invited me, and I ate some. Then we talked for awhile. Did you know he died before he came here, that he walked down a long tunnel and ended up in Silver Creek? He told me to put my hands on the mountain to remember more things. He said we should all do it. Remember like we did? He says the mountain has all the answers."

Kurt felt better. He hadn't seen his friend in so long, he had so much to say.

W.D. gazed up at the top of the mountain, bathed in yellow moonlight.

"I remembered who I was when my grandparents found me," said Kurt. "I couldn't remember my name, but I had found this name tag on the ground with the name Kurt written on it. I guess that's how I ended up with that name. But you know what? I think Roy Sharp and me are connected."

W.D. went up to the mountain and laid his hands on it.

"You know the donkey?" Kurt said. "His name is Shadow, same as Roy's donkey. Remember how all our horses ran off when we heard the gunshots? Well, Shadow came back to me. And you know how he found me? He had Roy's sneakers hanging from his neck. He smelled the sneakers and he must have followed the scent over to me." Kurt broke up, laughing. "He must have smelled my feet from across the desert!"

"Shh!" W.D. chided him. His eyes were closed, and he was clearly concentrating.

Kurt became quiet. The mountain had a power he did not want to disturb. It was important for W.D. to remember his life before Silver Creek.

He sat on a rock and waited. The dholes were still lying around, looking as if they had been tranquilized. He could no longer see their eyes.

Kurt wondered what had happened to George, Eddie, and all the others. He thought of how Daniel disappeared and hoped he was safe. All that time he spent updating W.D. about himself, he never thought to ask about their friends. For all he knew they could be in serious danger.

He went up to the mountain, stood beside W.D., and lay his hands on it. He was already quiet, so it didn't take long for the heat and the vibrations to kick in and juice up his body. It went straight down to his toes and filled him right up to the top of his head. The energy that thrilled him was so intense, it lit up the backs of his eyelids like sunlight.

Rather than waiting for a memory to form, he thought of George, Eddie, and the gang. He wanted to know where they were. Remembering that all the answers were in the mountains, Kurt asked it to help him.

Please, he said in his mind. Tell us where the others are, so we can find them.

He waited patiently for an answer. A picture flashed into his mind—a roller coaster with kids on it, raising their hands in the air and shrieking with glee. Then the image left his mind and he opened his eyes.

He saw something out of the corner of his eye. Just beyond the mountains to their north was the cresting hill of a roller coaster, decked in bright colored lights. But when he turned to look at it more closely, it shimmered and was gone.

Just then, W.D. climbed on top of one of the boulders. He grabbed hold of a short ledge just above his head and stepped up onto another boulder. Up and up he went.

Kurt followed him, although W.D. was faster. This mountain was a lot harder to climb than the one in Ohio. It was all bare rock with not many places to get one's footing. Kurt shadowed his friend as closely as possible, grabbing onto and stepping up on the same ledges.

But at one step, W.D.'s feet couldn't hold on, and he was hanging by his fingers. When he looked down, Kurt could see the pain and terror in his face.

"Help me!" It was the first time Kurt ever heard W.D. scream.

"Hang on, buddy!" Kurt shouted. "I'm coming!"

Kurt reached and pulled himself up to the next ledge. It was almost a vertical climb to where W.D. was hanging.

"Don't look down!" Kurt hollered. "Just hold on!"

W.D. was hanging by his fingertips, with his eyes closed, as if he were praying. "Hurry!" he cried.

Kurt kept moving, fighting the urge to look down. He kept his eyes on his friend and pushed himself higher and higher, until he reached the point where he was just below him.

"Step on my shoulders!" Kurt shouted.

The boy did. He was heavy, but Kurt had him in balance. He wasn't going to fall.

"We made it," said Kurt, who was gasping under the weight. "Are you all right, buddy?"

"I'm okay," W.D. answered between heaving breaths. "But how are we going to get down?"

"There's a ledge right where my fingers are," said Kurt. "I'm going to let you down just a little, and I want you to step on the ledge. Got that?"

"Got it." W.D. eased himself down to the ledge so that his feet were in Kurt's face. He wobbled, having nothing more than bare rock to hold onto.

Kurt held his hands up to steady him. "You're okay. I've got you," he said. "Now take another step down."

Kurt shadowed him from beneath, taking the same steps down one at a time. W.D. finally leaped down onto a flat, smooth ledge and met Kurt at eye level.

Kurt coughed to get the air back into his lungs. W.D.'s face was blotchy red, and he was trembling all over. He grabbed onto Kurt's shoulders and leaned his head into Kurt's chest. "Thank you," he said.

Kurt pushed him away gently. "What the heck were you doing up there?"

W.D. was still getting his breath back. "I got a picture in my mind, just like you said you did. I remembered being on a mountain when I first came into Silver Creek. In my mind I was climbing down, and when I fell, somehow I lost my voice. I remember being so scared, being alone, trying to figure out where I was. So, I whistled. It made me feel less scared."

"I was scared, too, when I first came here," said Kurt. "But now I just want to go back home. You didn't happen to get any other visions, did you? About your family, or where you came from?"

"I kept seeing this roller coaster, right out there." He pointed toward the northern sky, the same location where Kurt had seen it. "It must have been forty years ago that I last saw it. George still doesn't think I saw the roller coaster disappear back then."

"I just saw it," Kurt said. "I put my hands on the mountain and asked it to show me where the rest of gang is. In my mind I saw a roller coaster with kids on it. When I took my hands away, I saw the tip of the roller coaster just past the mountains. Then it disappeared."

W.D. looked astonished. "That's why I went looking for you. To tell you where we'd all been. We'd gone searching for you and Daniel. We found Daniel first, with his hands on a different mountain, way out there." He pointed toward the northern mountains.

"But how did he get there?" Kurt asked.

"He told us Miss Ruth's bird had landed on his shoulder and brought him there. Then right before our eyes, the mountain disappeared, and we saw that roller coaster. I had to find you so I could tell you."

"Tell me? How?" said Kurt. "You couldn't talk until you almost killed yourself climbing this mountain."

"Well, you went on and on for so long about the donkey and Mr. Jackson, and da-dit-da-dit-da-dit, I couldn't have said anything even if I wanted to!"

Kurt felt like slugging him, at first. "I do not go, da-dit-da-dit-da-dit."

"Yes, you do. You're worse than a broken record."

W.D. jumped down from the ledge, and quickly climbed down the rest of the mountain. Kurt tailgated him to the bottom. They walked right past the sleeping dogs and out into the darkness of the desert.

"Couldn't anyone come up with a better name for you than Whistling Dixie?" said Kurt.

"Bet you can't guess my real name," said W.D.

"It's probably something weird, like Wilbur. Right?"

"Wrong."

"Give me a hint."

"Nope."

17.

It had been a very long night. Now it was almost dawn. Cracks of daylight were just beginning to form over the eastern mountains, and soon the entire sky was washed in a lilac tint.

The very tip of the roller coaster was visible behind the western mountains. Silver Creek, which lay off in the other direction, looked empty and still.

All Kurt wanted was to get back home and sleep in his soft, comfortable bed. His eyes were little more than narrow slits, and his limbs felt heavy and awkward. He wouldn't have minded a change of clothes either. The desert world was starting to wear on him.

He heard the slow rhythm of hoof beats from behind. Shadow, sneakers still draped around his neck, was nodding as he strode toward the boys.

"What did I tell you?" said Kurt. "This guy would find me anywhere."

"Think we can both fit on him?" said W.D. "If I walk any farther, I think my legs will fall off."

At first, the donkey staggered under their combined weight. But he made no complaint and carried his heavy cargo toward the mountains.

How they both ever slept sitting up while riding a donkey, Kurt would never understand. But the next thing he knew, it was morning, and the donkey had come to a stop in front of the mountains. Both boys slid off their mount and collapsed onto the ground, where they slept away the early morning hours.

When Kurt woke up, W.D. was scrounging in the saddlebag, and chewing on food scraps.

"This meat is still pretty good," he said.

Kurt got up and rubbed his eyes, helping himself to a handful of the meat scraps. They were dry and tough to chew. "So when are you going to tell me your real name?"

"Later."

Just then, Kurt heard a dull roaring sound. At first it sounded like a distant avalanche. But then he saw a cloud of dust rising from the ground and the sound grew into a thundering of hoof beats. Then he heard gunshots, those same rumbling gunshots he'd heard the day before.

"It's time," W.D. said, pushing down the last piece of stale meat. "That's got to be the officials."

"What do we do?" Kurt asked.

W.D. went up to the mountain and put his hands on it, and Kurt did the same. W.D. had his eyes closed, so Kurt closed his, too.

First came the warm heat. Slowly, like molasses.

"Come on, come on, come on," Kurt said. But the more he tried to hurry the process, the slower the heat flowed through him.

The rushing sound of the charging army grew louder. Kurt tried to block out all his fear. Just get us past this mountain, he said in his mind. He thought of the roller coaster and the kids on the other side.

Then came the vibrations, traveling throughout his body. And just like instant developing film, his mind slowly etched a full color image of the kids

100

and the roller coaster. The picture in his mind was so perfect, it was as if they were all standing right in front of him.

The vibrations intensified so much, that the ground under his feet began to shake. When he opened his eyes, the mountain was trembling. A rock tumbled to the ground by their feet.

The boys backed away from it for fear that the mountain would crush them in a heap of stones. The din of the quake drowned out the sound of the approaching army.

Before their eyes, the mountain began to fade into a thin curtain through which they could see the shadow of the roller coaster, and all the kids— George, Eddie, Haley Dawn, Tiffany, Hoochie, Stephen, and Daniel. They were all standing together as if they were watching the event from their side.

Kurt and W.D. stepped up and put their hands right through the curtain.

"I think we can walk through," Kurt said.

"On the count of three," W.D. said. "One, two, three!"

Together they stepped through the curtain. It was as easy as crossing a threshold.

The seven kids gawked at them in awe. Kurt looked back and could still see the army charging toward them at full speed.

"Everyone on the roller coaster," Kurt said.

George looked as if he thought Kurt had lost his marbles. "Now? Are you crazy? They're coming right for us!"

Kurt yanked George's arm and pulled him after him. He shouted back to the others, "Let's go! We don't have much time!"

"I can run by myself. You can let go!" said George.

Kurt ran at full speed toward the roller coaster. It looked a lot like the one in Milky Way Park. Its peaks were almost as high as the mountains and the whole thing spiraled and sprawled like a giant at rest. It seemed so out of place, all by itself in the desert.

On the ground floor of the contraption was a train of passenger cars connected in the shape of a long spaceship. Kurt ushered all the kids into their seats and lowered their safety gear into place.

The mountain had nearly fully materialized, and the clamor of hoof beats had faded to a dull roar. Kurt watched as the mountain gradually regained its position, forming an impenetrable barrier. He listened. The noise had completely stopped.

"Thank you," he said aloud. But he wasn't sure to whom he had said it.

"Are we going to ride this thing today or not?" George called to him.

Kurt studied the roller coaster, and checked the ground floor. He walked all the way around the spaceship train.

"What's the matter?" George asked.

"I'm looking for a power switch," Kurt answered.

"Just get in," W.D. said.

"What do you know? He talks!" Hoochie cried.

"I didn't think he could talk," said Haley Dawn.

"But who'll get us moving?" Kurt asked.

"Just get on the stupid ride," said George. "We don't have all day."

Kurt climbed into the last car, where he sat by himself. Hoochie and Stephen were in the first car,

102

rocking themselves with excitement. Eddie sat with
Daniel, and Haley Dawn with Tiffany. George and
W.D. were in front of Kurt.

"Okay, now what?" Kurt asked.

"Maybe if W.D. whistles a song for us, this ride
will start moving," said Eddie.

"Yeah, come on, pal," said George. "Time for a
little motion music."

"Hmm, okay," said W.D.

Everyone waited for him to start. But the more
he thought, the more preoccupied he seemed to be.

"What's wrong?" Kurt asked.

"Did you forget how to whistle, W.D.?" Hoochie
asked.

"My name is Walter," W.D. said. "Walter
Cunningham."

Everyone turned and looked at him.

He closed his eyes, as if an answer were forming
in his mind. "I'm from Lakeview, Ohio. My parents
are David and Carol. I have a dog named Scottie.
We have a swimming pool in our backyard. And I
was on a roller coaster like this one when I last saw
them."

A long silence passed. Faces looked shocked, not
from fear, but from a sudden confusion that comes
when one finally learns the truth.

George patted him on the knee. "You're brave,
man."

One by one, the others started to verbalize their
memories. The group gradually became more at
ease in revealing their hidden pasts.

But Kurt had been only half-listening, because
his own memories were brewing inside him like
magma in a volcano. He did not feel brave. He was

afraid that if they all came pouring out at once, they would burn him like lava.

"Do you remember who you are?" Haley Dawn asked him.

Kurt felt self-conscious as they all turned to face him.

"I used to be Roy Robinson. My parents had a park called Robinson's Old West. I disappeared from it when I was five. There was a little yellow roller coaster there called the Bullet. That's the last thing I remember before I found myself in Silver Creek.

"People here called me Roy Sharp. But something inside me felt lonely. I was missing someone. And I got on my donkey, and went riding, looking for that missing someone, whoever it was.

"Somehow I ended up in a strange place. It seemed like a big amusement park. This lady, Mrs. Robinson, found me, and bought me an ice cream when she saw I was alone and scared."

The story began unraveling for him like a ball of yarn. He took a breath and continued.

"I didn't know my name when she asked me, but I found a name tag on the ground with the name Kurt. She went to find out where my mother was, but no one by the name of Kurt had been missing. So she took me home, and she and Pa raised me for awhile. Then their daughter Helen and her husband Cliff Van Loon adopted me, and brought me to see my grandparents every chance they could."

There was a thoughtful silence.

"So your grandparents are really your parents?" Eddie asked.

George turned to him in amazement. "That means your mom is really your sister!"

Kurt pondered the image of being older than his mom, but still being only thirteen. The thought of being his mom's big brother made him snicker.

The faces of the others broke into grins and they all started to laugh with him. Kurt felt like he was being tickled all over. He threw his head back and laughed so hard, he couldn't stop.

Faces turned beet red, cheeks were smeared with tears. Heads bent over the backs and sides of the cars, and the palms of their hands slapping one another.

The ride began to move along the track.

The laughing stopped, and the children all sat stunned as the train started itself and made its way around the first corner and began its ascent up the first major mountain of steel and girder.

Beyond the clacking of metal gears, Kurt thought he could still hear their laughter echoing from the mountains. It was a beautiful sound.

The roller coaster brought them up so high, Kurt thought he could touch the clouds. The ride crested at the top of the hill, pausing just long enough for Kurt to catch a final glimpse of Silver Creek. The children raised their hands high in the air, as the coaster went barreling down the other side. To Kurt it felt like he would never stop falling.

18.

The next thing Kurt knew, he was on his back, alone and gazing up at blue sky. His hand touched cool, smooth rock. The wind whispered something warm against his cheek.

He pushed himself up slowly to a sitting position. Looking down at the valley, he saw all of Milky Way Park, quiet and still. The grassy base of the mountain was far below.

Then he remembered, it was the same mountain he'd climbed to make his birthday wish.

He began his slow hike down. Hardy plants brushed up against him in the breeze. Birds chirped and fluttered from branch to branch. He was alone, but it was a different kind of aloneness. He felt protected.

He wondered what day it was. He had been in Silver Creek for three days. Or at least it felt that way. Had he just passed out on the mountain moments before and awakened?

The kids. He remembered George and W.D. and the rest of the gang so vividly. He remembered getting on the roller coaster with them, laughing with them. It couldn't have possibly been simply a journey of his imagination. It had felt all too real. Strange, but real.

Kurt took the shortest route back to Ma and Pa's house—a trail through the woods, then across the state highway, and through a field of high grass to Putnam Road.

When he arrived at the front steps, he opened the door quietly and heard Ma on the phone in the kitchen. All he could see was the phone cord stretched across the doorway.

"Say that again, Carol," she said into the phone. "Who's back? Your son Walter? Your son Walter who's been missing for forty years has come back, and he hasn't aged a day?"

Kurt stood rock still. This had to have been the same Walter from Silver Creek—W.D.

"Carol, honey, this long distance call is going to cost you a fortune. Maybe you just better go see a doctor. People our age are very prone to Alzheimer's."

Just as Ma appeared in the doorway, she caught sight of Kurt. She had a look of shock, anger, and relief, all rolled into one.

"You say my Kurt found him and seven other children? In a place called Silver Creek? How did he...? A roller coaster. Milky Way Park?" Her look softened into one of curious confusion. "Carol, I'm going to have to call you back." She hung up the phone and hurried right over to Kurt and threw her arms around him.

Kurt squeezed her tightly, burying his face in her shoulder.

"You've been gone for three days, Kurt. Pa and I have been worried sick about you. I called the police two days ago. I wasn't ready to live through that whole ordeal of losing a child again." She pulled away from him and held his face. "Are you all right? You look like you've been sleeping on a rock."

Kurt swallowed and nodded. He remembered the photo in his shirt. He took it out and showed it to Ma.

107

She was transfixed. "Why, this picture has to be fifty years old. But I don't recall having a silver frame for it." She turned it over and read the name on the back. "Dan Calloway?"

Kurt shuddered. He wasn't ready to tell Ma about Silver Creek, the mystery Pa told about many times, that she still wouldn't believe.

"Ma," he said, touching her arm, "what would you say if I told you I might be Roy?"

Ma looked as if she'd been shaken awake. "You mean like reincarnation? When someone dies, and instead of going to heaven they become another person?"

"No, I don't mean that," said Kurt. "Remember when you found me in Milky Way Park when I was five? You saw me crying because I'd spilled my ice cream, and you went and brought me another. You found that name tag on the ground with the name Kurt on it, and you said, 'Is this your name?'"

Ma had that same look Pa always had when he wanted to say something but couldn't. For a moment, that look frightened Kurt.

"Ma?" he said.

She set down the picture, and took Kurt in her arms and drew him close.

"Kurt, honey," she said. "You can't be anyone but yourself. You may have Roy's features. You may have even lived his life, as you say you did. But no one else could be my Kurt." She gave him a noisy, wet kiss on the cheek. "When Roy was here, I loved Roy. But now you're here, and I love you."

Just then, they heard a strained groan coming from the porch. It sounded like Pa was in pain.

"Coming, Pa!" Ma called. Kurt hurried after her.

When they stepped onto the porch, they both gasped at what they saw.

Pa was standing. His knees were bent slightly, and he was holding on to the porch railing, and looking out onto the yard.

"Shadow," he said in a muffled voice.

Kurt couldn't believe it. "Pa," he said.

Pa pointed a finger at the window. "Abby," he said.

Pa was talking. His speech was slurred, but he was talking.

Ma put her hands on top of his. She tried to smile, but her face had wrinkled up with tears. "Say something else, Pa."

Pa drew his hands away and pointed again out the window. "Shadow," he said again.

Kurt gazed out the window. There was a donkey in the backyard, sneakers draped around its neck.

"It is Shadow," Kurt said. He pushed open the screen porch door and stepped out into the yard.

Kurt stood still, not wanting to scare Shadow off. The donkey approached him slowly, its head bowed, and stopped at Kurt's side.

Kurt stroked the donkey's soft gray hair. He reached into the saddlebag and found a t-shirt which, when he unfolded it, displayed the words "Robinson's Old West" in faded red letters.

Christopher Doyle

Epilogue

Kurt climbed Mount Catawalla on his fourteenth birthday. This year he took his time. When he reached the summit, he had a sweeping view of Milky Way Park. He shivered with pleasure at the sound of delighted shrieks from riders on the Big Dipper roller coaster.

Sitting on the rock, he reflected on the events of the past year: the front-page article in the city newspaper about the return of eight missing children; the reunion picnic with his eight young friends from Silver Creek and their now elderly parents; his voice deepening; the short-lived surge of popularity he enjoyed at school; a free life-time admission ticket to Milky Way Park; his feet growing two more sizes; Pa's complete recovery from his stroke, except for some paralysis in his left hand; and the opening of the Aberdinery, a pastry shop run straight from Ma's kitchen and into the homes of Cockles Ridge and the surrounding counties.

But perhaps the most important event, the one that astounded him to this day, was the one that occurred around the same time that the front-page article appeared in the newspaper. He received a visit from a librarian in Columbus, a young woman named Joan Sharp. After reading the newspaper article about Kurt finding the missing children, she came right away to show Kurt the birth and marriage certificates of her great-great-great-great-great aunt Patsy who came from Ohio and traveled with her new husband Dan Calloway into the unsettled territory of Nevada in search of gold and silver. Distant relatives of Patsy passed on the story that she and Dan had had a very troubled marriage. Dan took his life after losing a fortune in silver, and Patsy became a recluse and died childless.

As Kurt listened to Joan's story, he remembered the silver frame. He excused himself and ran up to Ma and Pa's bedroom to retrieve it. When he showed it to Joan and directed her attention to Dan Calloway's signature, she stared at it in amazement.

"I found it in Silver Creek," Kurt told her.

"What's Silver Creek?" Joan asked. And so he told her the story of how he magically appeared in the Old West town.

Joan chuckled. "I suppose you have to see it to believe it," she said.

"No," Kurt said, smiling mysteriously at her. "You have to believe it to see it."

About the Author

Christopher Doyle was inspired to write for children during his student teaching. Since then he has shared his enthusiasm for writing with hundreds of fourth-graders, and has inspired some to become future authors.

The Silver Creek Secret is the author's first novel for children. He teaches at St. Joseph School in Salem, Massachusetts, where he resides.

Printed in the United States
1237200001B/37-60

9 781410 707147